LOVER'S CHRISTMAS

A Ramsey Tesano Novella

BY

ALTONYA WASHINGTON

LOVER'S CHRISTMAS

A Ramsey Tesano Novella

Copyright © 2012 by AlTonya Washington

ISBN 13: 978-0982978184

Printed in USA by Createspace LLC

To my amazing Ramsey and Tesano Addicts. I hope this will be an enjoyable 'fix'.

Happy Holidays!

CHAPTER ONE

The exclusive gated Seattle neighborhood that Quaysar and Tykira Ramsey called home was; for the most part, a peaceful locale. That is, unless the Ramsey couple was holding one of their highly anticipated barbeques, Parents Only movie nights or play dates for their sons Dinari and Dakari.

While the neighborhood was home to over a dozen young couples, Quay and Ty harbored the majority of the popularity. The couple was always happy to host social events be they all inclusive or of the more intimate variety.

It went without saying that Quay had definitely adopted the 'family man' mantra and he wore it with pride. Of course no one was more surprised than Quay. Furthermore, no one was more pleased.

Quest Ramsey was most definitely pleased and he was not above telling his brother how much. Quay knew his twin well though and he understood that Quest had to keep saying that to prove to himself that he wasn't dreaming it.

~~~

Like mirror images of chocolate-dipped perfection, the brothers sat on opposite ends of a charcoal gray suede sectional sofa. They took in the last quarter of the Seahawks game they had placed bets on with their cousins.

Quay's adopted twin sons were in their own world having taken over the huge black and tan checkered rug set in front of where their father and uncle relaxed on the sofa. The boys crashed into each other's trucks, making all the necessary rumbling engine and booming noises that boys felt they needed to make in order to bring more realism into their play.

"Dammit!" Quay bellowed with a resounding clap as he leaned forward on the sofa. "Come on you muthafuckas!" he raged as the defense set up for another play.

The twins turned to their father, surprise and humor lacing their cute milk-chocolate toned faces.

Quay winked at his sons. "Shh…" he placed a finger over his mouth. "Don't tell mommy."

The boys tumbled back on the rug and rolled with laughter before returning to their play.

Grinning and sparking a deep right dimple, Quay relaxed back on the sofa again. He caught a glimpse of his twin's face and fixed him with a probing look. "What's up?" he queried.

"What?" Quest raised his broad shoulders in a brief shrug.

Quay rolled his eyes. "Don't even try it…is it the trip?"

Grinning and sparking a deep *left* dimple, Quest threw up his hand in a dismissive wave. "As usual I don't know what the hell you're talkin' about."

"I know the timing's piss poor but when *isn't* the timing piss poor in this family?" Quay went on as though his brother hadn't voiced his confusion. "It's probably the last time Tyke's doctor will give her the okay to travel like this."

Quest's smile that time was softer as he detected the underlying concern in his brother's voice. "The trip's a good idea," he knocked a fist against Quay's denim-clad knee when he leaned across the sofa. "Mick and I could sure as hell use it," he reclined on the sofa then as well, massaging his eyes with the heels of his hands.

Quay forgot about the game. Concern had turned his already ebony stare an impossibly deeper shade of onyx. "You guys okay?" he asked.

Still massaging his eyes and reclining on the sofa, Quest smiled. "We're good. It's nothing like what you're thinking."

"So? What is it?"

"You think we could have the 'big talk' *after* the holidays?" Quest leaned forward then, resting an elbow to his knee in order to begin a new massage at his neck.

Unfortunately, the words 'big' and 'talk' told Quaysar all he needed to know. "Is it as bad as it sounds?"

"No," Quest moved the massage deeper into the raised collar of his slate green fleece top. "I'm sure it's much worse."

"Shit," Quay hissed, his voice too low for the boys to overhear. "Should we even be going on this trip then?"

"Yeah," Quest winced regretting that he'd given his brother cause for concern. "Yeah, it's fine." He gave Quay the benefit of his steady gaze then. "We're good. It'll be an early Christmas for the big kids and I'm definitely ready to have a little fun with my toy." He voiced the last, once he'd leaned back against the sofa again.

"Hmph," Quay mimicked his brother's action and lovingly observed the playing boys on the rug. "These guys are my heart, but it'll be fun to have their mommy all to myself for a few days."

One of Tykira's adoring clients had decided to make a Christmas gift of his newly renovated ski resort set to reopen just after the New Year. He'd offered to open his doors for a week or however long Ty and her guests wanted to stay.

It was all in thanks for the work Ty and her team had put in on the client's upcoming retirement community in Vermont. Ty's expert listening skills enabled her to transfer the client's wishes to a tee in the plans she and her architects created. Ty had assured her clients that the eye popping fees they'd paid out to she and her staff were thanks enough.

Alas, the clients insisted. Ty couldn't deny that the resort was to die for. Besides, she and her husband craved just one last jaunt before all travel was forbidden. Therefore, the Ramseys extended the invitation for a couple's holiday and received an *almost* unanimous acceptance.

"You really think it's alright to leave the kids and everybody else behind?"

Quest knew Quay was referring to the as yet unconquered threat from Evangela Leer and her crew.

"Moses has his guys on us," Quest rested his elbows to his knees and studied his hands rubbing one inside the other. "A unit will be camped out here at your place with Ma, Dad and the kids. They're even three guys with Ms. Bobbie at her place," he referred to Ty's mother Roberta Lowery. "Same goes for Aunt Josephine," he shrugged and slanted a look toward Quay.

"I'd say we're as covered as we can be. Moses even had a crew fly ahead to the resort to make sure everything checks out with Ty's clients. We've got people on Uncle West, Aunt Bri, Aunt Georgia," Quest ticked the names off on his fingers and then grinned.

"What?" Quay probed with a half-smile curving his mouth.

"Not sure we'll really need folks on Aunt G. Uncle Felix says he's got her in check."

Quay threw back his head and laughed. "Uncle Felix is the man," he raved before a more sobering look crept over his face. "You heard from 'Los and Dena?"

The question turned Quest's expression darker. In light of the fact that he'd yet to speak with his cousin Dena and her husband Carlos McPhereson; about new and disturbing facts he'd recently been made aware of, their recent disappearing act felt even more jarring.

"It's weird," Quest gave his head a clearing shake.

"Has Taurus heard anything?" Quay referred to their cousin and Dena's younger brother.

Again, Quest shook his head. "Not since Carlos called out of the clear blue and said he was taking her out of town. He didn't say where he was taking her." Quest answered the question he knew his twin was gearing up to ask. The den door opened then and he celebrated the interruption.

Tykira Lowery leaned against the door frame looking impossibly lovely and vibrant despite the fact that she was in her second trimester. "Hey guys, they're here," she patted a hand to the middle of her hooded mauve sweatshirt where her stomach protruded. "We'll be ready to head out to the airstrip as soon as Kraven gives the kids their presents."

"Presents?!" Dinari and Dakari cried in gleeful unison. Without a second thought, they abandoned the wealth of toys on the big rug to go in search of newer ones.

Ty laughed, giving her racing five year old sons a wide berth as she held the den door open.

Again, Quay noticed the look on Quest's face as Quest watched his nephews barrel out of the room. "What the hell is it, man?" Quay asked.

Quest's laughter carried on a more robust chord. "I'm good, I promise."

"Oh, I get it…" Quay let his obsidian gaze narrow in a sly, playful manner. "You're the odd man out with two women to handle, right?"

That time, Quest's smile and resulting laughter were thoroughly genuine. "If *that's* what it means to be the odd man out, then I'll take it any day."

Quay followed suit when his brother pushed off the sofa. "So does Michaela know how much you want another baby?"

Quest hung his head and accepted that it was sheer foolishness to continually put up a front for the man who; with the exception of his wife, knew him better than anyone.

"Quincee's everything to me," he swore.

Quay's smile reflected understanding. "And you love her so much, you want to give her some company."

"Jesus Quay," Quest massaged his eyes again. "No heavy stuff for this trip, alright?"

Without hesitation, Quay nodded his agreement and then kissed his twin's cheek and pulled him into a hug.

~~~

Ty wasn't the only one eager for one last trip before the…joys of pregnancy made it a chore to put one foot before the other.

Darby DeBurgh had literally begged her husband for the trip. She knew that; given the man's unreasonably overprotective nature, he'd probably not be willing to let her venture to the bathroom once she started to show.

Kraven didn't bother telling his wife that begging wasn't necessary. He was just as eager for a leisurely couple's retreat, especially given the circumstances surrounding their last gathering. Of course, he knew and appreciated all too well the joys of being the recipient of his wife's 'begging' and he let her have at it.

The DeBurghs arrived at Quay's and Ty's loaded down with brightly wrapped packages. Everyone was clearly feeling the holiday season perhaps a bit more than need be given that Christmas was still over a month away. Nevertheless; as the glee and optimism were hard to come by as of late, no one begrudged giving in to a bit of premature merriment.

Taurus, Nile, Kraven and Darby were the last couples to arrive. Others had trekked in earlier that afternoon or the previous evening all ready to get the trip underway.

Dinari and Dakari were understandably the happiest to greet the late arrivers. The little boys' big brown eyes sparkled with expectancy when Kraven knelt before them and set down the huge bag he'd carried in slung across his shoulder.

"Hope you're gonna stick around to help me build the extra room we're gonna need to store all this stuff," Quay told Kraven once he'd hugged him and Taurus and accepted simultaneous cheek-kisses from Nile and Darby.

"Between you and these folks we could open up a store," Quay went on, that time referring to Damon, Catrina and Bobbie. The grandparents looked on as expectantly as their grandsons toward the wrapped presents.

"Don't listen to him Kraven," Ty laughed, "you guys should see how overboard some *fathers* go."

Quay merely shrugged and appeared indifferent.

None of it mattered to the little twins. They clapped and posted up on their sneakers as Kraven made a big show of pulling out all the gifts.

"Alright lads, gather 'round," Kraven inclined his head as though he intended to share a secret with the toddlers.

Eagerly, the boys jostled closer.

"If it's okay with your mom and dad, you guys can open one of these tonight," Kraven leaned in a bit closer and patted the bag. "The rest go under the tree 'til the big day."

"Mommy?" Dinari and Dakari spoke in unison, immediately turning pleading eyes to Tykira and then tugging on Quay's jeans.

The parents pretended to mull over the decision and then allowed the deal. The boys clapped hysterically and then followed Kraven's instructions to cart the presents from the foyer to place them under the tree. Once the job was done, they settled around the wide ten-footer to decide which gift to open first.

Kraven wasn't done with his gift giving however. In addition to their own presents, the twins had carried in items for Quincee who would also be staying at her aunt and uncle's home along with her grandparents and cousins while her parents were away.

For the little girl who had captured his heart, Kraven brought an extra special gift. Quincee had stood around with her cousins when Kraven and the others had arrived. She appeared just as gleeful as the boys although she didn't fully understand what all the fuss was about. The brightly wrapped packages however were enough to make anyone's eyes widen.

Quincee ambled over to Kraven when he beckoned to her with an extended hand. Her expressive gray eyes shimmered with excitement and she giggled when he hugged her tenderly and kissed one of her plump cocoa brown cheeks.

With theatric slowness, Kraven ventured into the nearly empty red sack. Quincee's baby-toothed grin emerged and her tiny hands came together in a quiet happy clap at the sight of the handmade rag doll Kraven produced. Everyone laughed when she hugged the toy close.

Quincee was kissing Kraven's cheek to thank him as the twins returned to the foyer with their early opened trucks in hand.

Nile laughed and then leaned close to Darby. "Hope you've got a girl in there," she patted a hand to her best friend's still-flat belly.

The twins overheard the comment and appeared terribly dismayed.

"No more girls!" They said.

The room roared with laughter. Everyone understood what had roused the boys' distress. A week earlier, Tykira had announced to the family that she and Quay would soon be adding twin girls to the Ramsey foal.

***

One of the Ramsey jets had been fueled and prepped to carry the group on their journey to the Wakefield Resort located amidst the Green Mountains in Vermont. A relaxing ride on the plush jet was one of the reasons Ty's doctor had given the trip his blessing.

The same was true for Sabella who; while not as far along as Ty, was still being carefully watched by her doctor given her previous medical scare resulting from a carelessly prescribed medication.

Isak and Sabella Tesano resided on the East coast. They had been out West seeing to the Monterrey California home owned by Belle's mother Carmen Ramsey. Carmen was getting settled in her new life with her new husband and old flame Jasper Stone. The Tesanos had ventured up to Seattle to spend the day with Quest and Mick before the Vermont trip.

Fernando Ramsey along with his brothers Yohan and Moses merely had to drive a few minutes to arrive with their wives at Quay's and Ty's since they all resided in Seattle as well.

Sabra Ramsey was last to arrive in her typical diva fashion. Everyone was thankful; though they dared not admit it too loudly, that Sabra's fiancé Smoak Tesano was able to take a break from his work to join them and to keep an eye on his fiery wife-to-be.

Once the group was settled; in the decadently plush sable brown seats furnishing the massive cabin, drinks of all types were provided by the attentive flight staff. Soon, the vacationers were taking a moment to breathe and quietly anticipate the next several days. In spite of all the relaxing vibes, no one could miss the absence of Carlos and Dena.

"So I guess no one's the last bit worried about that?" Sabra asked in a huff while she kicked off the hemp colored platform heels she wore with skin tight jeans of the same color. "Carlos just carrying her off like that, doesn't seem weird?"

Moses had long since kicked off his sneakers and was settled back in his seat. "Carlos is her husband in case you forgot that little detail." He told his younger cousin.

"And?" Sabra sniffed. "That doesn't give him the right to just whisk her away like that."

"Well hell girl, that's what we just did to y'all." Fernando reasoned coolly and received a slap to the back of his head from his wife.

"Thanks County," Sabra called from her side of the cabin where she was then curled up against Smoak on the sofa seat they shared.

"And anyway *Moses*," Sabra paused until his eyes opened to slits and he shifted the dark orbs in her direction. "It was Ty who got us the hook up and whisked us away." She raised a hand to silence any comeback from her cousin and turned back to Tykira. "So tell us about this place, girl."

Ty laughed when Moses rolled his eyes and resumed his relaxing pose. "Well um," she set her mug of whipped cream laced cocoa to a nearby end table. "It's been in my client's family for decades. It's high up in the Green Mountains of Vermont- they totally scrapped the old construction and rebuilt the place." Ty folded her hands atop her belly and swiveled her chair to and fro.

"It's the exact same model as the original place only with subtle modifications to make it a more state of the art establishment."

"State of the art, huh?" Sabra's stunning smoky gaze narrowed in sync with her dubious inquiry. The idea that any place could rival her wildly successful Las Vegas resort hotel casino seemed inconceivable to her. "What's a night go for?" She asked.

Tykira faked nonchalance and barely raised a hand from her stomach. "Your highest rollers probably couldn't afford a night there."

Quaysar and Fernando erupted into hearty, contagious laughter. Soon, everyone was joining in on the amusement.

Everyone except Sabra, who merely rolled her eyes closed.

***

The Green Mountains of Vermont were a 250 mile range just outside Montpelier. Part of the Appalachians, the Green Mountains were known to have phenomenal ski conditions during the winter and amazing hiking in the summer months.

Once the jet had set down at the airstrip, the group deplaned and headed for the array of Range Rovers. The vehicles would chauffer two couples per car to the Wakefield Resort via the easy to navigate access road which led up into the depths of the range.

While the car and aircraft crews combined efforts to move luggage from the jet to the Rovers, the couples met up in a semi-circle to enjoy the late afternoon view of the sun that beamed gloriously behind the snow covered mountains. Silence reigned as the group reveled in the utter beauty before their eyes.

The flight captains walked over to shake hands with the men and to engage in a few last minute conversations before they bid the group a good trip and promised to see them during the return flight to Seattle.

Michaela had hung close to the men instead of strolling toward the SUVs with the women. She waited until her husband broke away from the group to pull him aside.

"Have you told them what we found out?" she nodded toward the rest of the guys when Quest dropped an arm about her shoulders.

He kept her close, warming a hand against the heavy wine colored fleece of her jacket when he rubbed her back. "I told Quay not to ask me about it until after the trip."

Mick's brows raised a notch. "You think that's a good idea with 'idiot Leer' and her crew still on the loose?"

Quest grinned, tugging at one of his wife's windblown onyx curls. "I feel good about having Mo's guys looking over our shoulders."

"Right," Mick sighed, "and what about the *top man* suddenly venturing off to parts unknown with his wife?"

"I can't let myself think it's anything negative." Quest shrugged beneath the thick black and gray chambray jacket he wore. "At least not until after the trip."

Michaela could have continued with her speculations had she not been jerked into a smothering kiss just then. The gesture was utterly effective in clearing her mind of everything but the man who held her, raising her progressively higher against his tall, leanly chiseled frame. The kiss deepened and Mick; mindless to all else, boldly wrapped her legs around his waist and thrust her tongue repeatedly, feverishly against his.

The sound of cheers and claps of approval for the unintended show, reached the couple's ears. Michaela hid her face in the base of Quest's throat. Meanwhile, he grinned a wickedly arrogant grin for the raving crowd. Without relinquishing his hold on Mick, he joined the group at the Rovers.

"We make this trip off limits to discussing anything dramatic-deal?" Quest proposed.

Some said 'deal'. Others said 'Amen'. All were in agreement while settling into their respective cars.

~~~

As with everything related to the Ramseys and Tesanos however, drama; in one form or another, was a difficult thing to escape…

CHAPTER TWO

As Tykira had informed her guests earlier, the Wakefield Resort was a brand new construction having been built into a replica of the previous Wakefield Inn which had graced the massive acreage for decades.

Without the plain, unassuming wooden sign designating the turn off, travelers would drive right past, never realizing the beautiful establishment was nestled deep inside the mountain range.

Veering from the public access road, the trail became less smooth. Dirt and gravel laden in warmer months, snow covered during winter, the route could prove treacherous at any time of the year. One would have to be serious about a visit should they choose to continue along such a path. Once the uneven expanse was conquered, the trail opened out into an easier to navigate stretch of road that twisted deeper toward the destination.

Smoak and Sabra occupied the first Rover. Work laden as usual, even Smoak couldn't concentrate on much else beyond the beautiful scenery that beckoned his remarkable black stare. He uttered an impressed whistle while gazing down into the sea of snowy white that claimed everything around them. As far as the eye could see, the area was dotted by the tree tops pushing their way through the snow.

"Jeez, this is some view," he breathed. "Babe? You seein' this?"

Sabra was too busy slamming her mobile against the charcoal gray suede seating. "Damn phone. Where's my signal?"

"I think this is a vacation," he smirked over her dismay.

"And *I* think that vacations end," Sabra sweetly reminded the love of her life. "Work is forever."

"Hell, *that's* your outlook?" he was incredulous. "No wonder you're always so pissed about it."

"Pissed?"

One sleek brow drifted higher than the other and Smoak's expression appeared more amused. His dig had produced the desired response and had taken her mind off the phone.

"*You're* one to talk," Sabra used the phone to point his way. "How much work did *you* bring along? I know you've got it stashed someplace." She leered at him suspiciously. "Is it in the trunk?"

Shrugging lazily beneath a black three quarter length leather jacket, Smoak appeared at ease. "I've got it here inside the truck," he confessed.

"I knew it! You talk about *me*. Bet you'll be working every minute." She was turning back to her phone when she felt Smoak's hand hook the underside of her thigh. She shrieked when he dragged her flat on the seat and covered her with his lean, iron frame a mere few seconds later.

"Working the entire time? God I hope so..." his rich voice trailed off into her neck where he kissed her.

Work and anything else non-erotic fled Sabra's thoughts then. While she'd never been known for her shyness, she slid a look toward the front of the SUV and was happy to find that a wood-grained privacy panel had been raised to shelter their actions from the driver.

Smoak didn't seem to mind one way or another about onlookers. With one hand, he spread Sabra's thighs further apart so that he could settle himself more snuggly against her. He used his free hand to tug himself out of the heavy jacket. Sabra kissed him with a fiery eagerness, her fingers working rapidly over the dark buttons of the flannel black olive shirt he wore.

Smoak wasn't of a mind to share control just then however. Capturing Sabra's wrists, he drew them none-too-gently above her head. Once he'd doffed his jacket, he went to work on the fastening of her jeans. He'd wanted to get inside the unbelievably skin-tight creations since she'd slinked into them that morning.

Sabra lost her ability to match the vigorous thrusts of his tongue when she felt his thumb at work against her. He stroked the fleshly mound of her clit while his middle finger worked its way inside her rapidly moistening folds. Her body arched sharply, hips writhing to encourage him to move faster. She'd managed to free her wrists and undo his shirt in order to push her hands under the white T-shirt he wore beneath it. Her nails curved into the granite blackberry slab that was his chest in a silent demand for him to finger her more satisfactorily.

He refused of course, preferring to drive her mad with his skilled touch for just a few moments longer. Once his middle finger eased all the way home, Sabra thanked him with a throaty kiss and shaky moan of approval. She heightened her efforts when his index finger joined the play.

Somewhere in the back of the truck, Sabra's phone found a signal and began to chime.

"You're back in business," his voice was a growl; muffled, due to the fact that his sinfully beautiful face was buried in her chest.

"Screw it," Sabra growled back.

Chuckling then, Smoak raised up slightly to graze her earlobe with his perfect teeth. "Not quite what I had in mind…"

~~~

Smoak and Sabra had been the first to leave the airstrip but the last to arrive at the lodge where the Ramseys, Tesanos and DeBurghs would be the exclusive occupants aside from the skeleton lodge staff and additional security. Luggage had been placed in each couples' suite along with hot coffee, cocoa and tea for two. A fully stocked bar appeared in each suite for those desiring beverages with a bit more kick.

In addition to the wood-grained encased walled bars, each suite held a private balcony. The areas offered splendid views of the snowy grounds which were surrounded by breath-stealing mountains. A rooftop terrace was accessible via an outside facing elevator. The terrace could be enjoyed year-round and it provided yet another viewing advantage of the wintry atmosphere.

~~~

It took Michaela a while to be hit by the gorgeous environment as she was still rifling through her things and cursing herself for doing a half-assed job during her packing. Incessant searching for one item in particular slowed and then halted all together when a pair of arms encircled her waist.

Her breathing labored and all thoughts blurred as Quest nudged aside the curls bumping her neck to make room for his mouth to explore. Michaela felt her hands draining of strength, weakening over the luggage on the bed. Quest's persuasive and provocatively shaped mouth trailed around one side of her neck. She leaned back her head, bracing it against the muscular wall of dark chocolate drenched flesh beneath the gray and black checked shirt he wore outside sagging denims.

"Aren't we supposed to meet everybody downstairs?" her question sounded as weak as her hands felt.

"We've got time," his hands were already beneath her sweater and wrenching the white undershirt from the waistband of her khakis.

"I need to finish unpacking," her words were a soft moan.

In response, Quest took the duffle and dropped it to the floor. Seconds later, he had her in its place upon the four poster Maplewood king.

Mick was opening her mouth to say his name but Quest stifled her intentions with his kiss.

"Didn't have time to finish with you in the car," he freed her lips long enough to explain.

Mick felt her breath catch momentarily. "I um…I thought you finished with me quite nicely."

"Not enough," his voice was muffled due to his heart-stopping face presently masked beneath Michaela's sweater.

"Quest-"

He rose above her suddenly. With a singular tug, he relieved himself of the top shirt he wore. Mick was awestruck despite the many times she'd had the honor of gazing upon the perfection of his body. Reaching out, she grazed her fingertips along the captivating display of his abs. Biting down into the full curve of her lip, she swept her fingers upward until her thumbnail scraped his nipple. The pleasure roused from the simple touch incited her to perform a wicked grind on his thigh. Her lashes fluttered but she dared not close her eyes against the delicious flex of his pectorals.

Quest covered her again, the left dimpled grin emerging as he studied his wife's expression. Sheer elation surged through him just because she was near.

"Still concerned about the time?" He asked.

Dazed still, Mick focused on the lazy rotation her thumb was making over his dimple. "What time?" She murmured.

***

Eventually, all the couples were settled into their suites and ready to explore their expansive surroundings. Some were floored by the billiards room that was complete with flat screen TVs on every wall and showing a mix of sporting events.

Others decided that the outrageously over the top movie room would certainly get a workout. The resort unarguably catered to the most extraordinary tastes.

"Have y'all seen that hot tub room? We're definitely gonna have to find time to use that." Sabra was saying once she'd found the rest of the girls in the kitchen.

They had all collected in the sprawling state of the art space. Unfinished white oak cabinets, black granite countertops and stainless steel appliances gave the area a warm yet sophisticated aura.

"I saw it," Darby called while helping herself to one of the cream cheese pinwheels that had been provided by the cook staff and covered a large ceramic dish in the center of the kitchen island. "It'd be the perfect spot for me, Ty and Belle to have our baby shower."

Tykira; who was seated at the far end of the island that everyone had gathered around, burst into laughter.

Sabella presently filling Ty's glass with the virgin Pina Colada she'd mixed, only shook her head.

"Now *that* would be a sight." Ty was still laughing.

"No…" Belle sighed and wiped the rim of the blender's pitcher. "The *sight* would be *me* tryin' to work my fat ass into a hot tub."

"Please shut the hell up." Sabra promptly ordered her lovely cousins. "Darby that's a great idea."

"I'll just give you your present *before* you waddle yourself down to the hot tub." Belle told Ty.

The two clinked glasses.

"No rush," Ty sipped the creamy perfectly mixed drink. "I plan to come down with a mysterious case of the sniffles that night."

"Would you guys reconsider if it was just us girls? Maybe we can get the guys out of the house that night." Johari suggested.

"Why do the guys have to leave?" Sabra asked and received the 'you're an idiot' look from the rest of the group.

"Do you really think they'd let us prance down to sit in hot tubs without them being part of it?" Mick asked, reaching for a third pinwheel.

"She's got a point," Nile offered up her glass for a bit of the pina colada. "We'd never make it out of the bedroom dressed or…undressed like that."

"Ah come on, the place is big enough to share." Melina reasoned, "We could tell 'em we want a girl's night and ask if they could find something to do on the other side of the house or outside of it for a few hours."

The skeptics exchanged shrugs.

"Could work," Belle said.

"Then, it's a date," Contessa decided and grabbed five of the pinwheels from the glazed lime green plate.

The group of beauties stood in silence for a while and munched enthusiastically on all the delectable treats provided by the very efficient and discrete cooks.

"So why do you guys think 'Los and Dena *really* aren't here?" Sabra asked once they'd polished off the pinwheel platter.

"Sabra, jeez…" Johari rolled her eyes. "Let that go, please."

"Quest was right. No drama on this trip." County said.

"It's weird," Sabra stubbornly continued and tossed a lock of her almost waist length tresses across her shoulder. "De was so upset about not being able to go to Belle and Pike's wedding. Doesn't seem like Carlos would have an issue with being here. He can damn well vouch for the security staff, you know?"

Melina rested her elbows on the island and extended her hands. "What if this is one of those very rare times that it is what it is? No drama. No...hidden mystery?" She shrugged beneath the fuzzy apricot sweater she wore. "Maybe they just wanted to get away."

"Amen," County saluted with the last pinwheel on her napkin.

Everyone else voiced their agreement as well, cheering with whatever food or drink they held.

Sabra sniffed her disdain. "I still think it's weird," she muttered.

~~~

The distinct rumble of male voices filtered out past the lodge's main room. The immaculate space was golden lit, the gleam of it more potently defined by the rich wood work and the cream and burgundy color scheme.

Floor to ceiling windows occupied the rear wall of the room and spanned the entire four stories of the lodge. Beyond partly drawn curtains, the night skies were revealed and moonlight glinted off the snow laden grounds.

"Don't make me ask twice, Q." Taurus' exquisite champagne tinged eyes were hard and fixed on his cousin.

Quest slanted a threatening look toward his twin who had conspicuously headed to the bar and was taking longer than necessary to top off his gin.

"I could've sworn I said I wanted to talk about this *after* the trip." Quest spoke to Quay's back and waited for his brother to turn.

At last, Quay turned to face the music. "And that's exactly what I told T."

"Jesus Quay," Quest massaged his eyes then, their hazy gray color had transitioned to the inky black that hinted at the rise of his temper. It wouldn't take much more than the words 'big' and 'talk' to generate interest and suspicion ten times over. He looked back to Taurus.

"I'm not ready to say that I think Carlos taking Dena away is about anything other than him wanting to be alone with her."

"But something has you curious about it. What?" Moses asked from his end of the sofa he and Taurus occupied.

Kraven patted Quest's shoulder on his way to the bar. "Cat's already clawing at the bag, man as well go on and open it." He grinned.

Quay followed Kraven's expression by offering up an encouraging smile. He chuckled when his brother gave him the finger.

"I've had Drake Reinard looking into a financial matter." He referred to his CFO of Ramsey's European offices. "It looks like money's been leaving Uncle Houston's discretionary account at Ramsey World since after his death. They were funds only *he* had access to- ones only he was permitted to move. Drake was able to trace the leaking money back to Dena."

The rustle of fabric sounded as several of the men shifted uncomfortably in their seats.

"She *is* his daughter, Q." Yohan's heavy voice was next to fill the room. "Does Drake think she's up to something shady?"

"Nobody's saying that," Quest raised his hands and replaced them decisively on either arm of his chair. "But given everything that went on with your dad," he looked to Taurus. "It's a lot of money T. No one has a clue about where it went, but from what we've seen it doesn't look like De's kept any of it for herself."

"Shit," Quay set his elbows to his knees and smoothed his hands over the top of his head. "Man, I'm sorry Q." At last, he understood why his brother wanted the discussion to wait.

Quest left his chair to join Kraven at the bar. There, he helped himself to a generous refill of Bourbon.

"So what now?" Pike was asking from his leaning stance against one of the built in Birchwood bookshelves along the far wall.

Quest observed his old friend and frat brother for an exaggerated moment. Silently, he gave thanks that he hadn't hinted to Quay what he and Michaela had discovered about Pike's father-in-law Jasper Stone.

"I say, right now it'd be best to leave it all in this room. If everyone's good with that?" Quest sent a pointed look toward his mirror image.

"Yeah," Quay's grimace ignited his right dimple and he nodded. "Hell yeah…"

"This is gonna be fun," Smoak groaned rolling up the sleeves of his dark shirt. His voice signaled how little he was looking forward to quelling his fiancée's queries about her cousin's impromptu trip.

Fernando; whose chair faced the room's entrance, grinned. "Speak of the devil- it's the bride to be."

"Have we interrupted your plotting?" Sabra asked as she arrived in the room ahead of the other women.

"Jeez girl, have you *always* been this suspicious?" Quay fanned out the lightweight Carolina blue sweatshirt he wore and frowned at his cousin.

Sabra wasn't put off in the least. "Come off it. You guys always find a way to get together and conspire."

While Quay merely waved her off, Sabra took note of the men's somber faces. "Were you just comparing notes on Carlos and Dena?" She asked in a poorly disguised attempt to sound nonplussed.

Melina laughed and took her place on Yohan's lap. "Girl, *you* are the only one who's taken any notes."

"So what gives?" Sabra eased her hands into the back pockets of her skin tight denims. "I know I'm not the only suspicious one around here?"

Smoak left his chair, expressing a long sigh as he stood. He crossed to where Sabra stood and pulled her close.

"We were talking about how we're gonna miss Carlos and Dena since this has the makings of a damned good vacation." He dropped a lingering kiss to her ear. "I know we can both use it," he added.

"Amen to that," Moses said, squeezing Johari's thigh when she sat on the arm of the sofa.

"Well I just-"

"Babe?" Smoak patted Sabra's hip and squeezed. "Forget about all the rest." Again, he slid his mouth to her ear.

Sabra swallowed noticeably and mellowed instantly.

The remaining guests looked on in amazement as the engaged couple made their way from the room.

"I'm lovin' you more and more every day, man." Quay remarked as the couple passed behind his chair. "We've been trying to figure out how to shut her up for years."

Smoak revealed a sly grin. Sabra applied a resounding slap to the back of her cousin's head. Laughter abounded and then the rest of the couples decided to call it a night as well.

CHAPTER THREE

There was a late start to things the next morning. The kitchen had been designated as the meeting place and slowly the residents of the Wakefield Lodge began to amble in. Some were still yawning as they awakened to the wondrous aromas of fresh brewed coffee, tea or cocoa.

Tykira's tastes ran differently. Upon her arrival in the kitchen, she headed to the refrigerator in search of milk. The double sided stainless-steel appliance held every delectable imaginable it seemed.

The Wakefield Lodge thought of everything for its guests. The cook staff provided elaborate dinners and appetizers. Lunches and breakfasts were available at the guests' request should they opt not to cook for themselves, sample from the resort's exquisite eateries or venture into the town to try the restaurants located there.

Ty's search of the refrigerator had taken her to the lower shelving. She was on her knees, the bottom of her fuzzy gold robe brushing the floor, as she read the nutrition information on the back of a yogurt container when husband arrived.

"Dammit Tyke," Quay bounded over to pluck his wife from the floor as though she were weightless. "What the hell are you doin'?" He asked once he'd set her on one of the oversized cushioned chairs in the alcove.

"I was just," Ty pointed weakly toward the fridge, "looking for the milk."

He muttered something and shook his head as he took position on the coffee table before the chair.

"Hey?' She waited for him to look up. "I'm not an invalid." Smiling, she brushed her fingers across his devastating indigo eyes hoping to ease the worry she found lurking there.

"Did you sleep?" She asked.

"Were you in bed with me?" he countered.

"Yes."

"Then I slept better than I ever have in my life."

Their sweet kiss turned lusty in the span of a minute. Ty was seconds away from suggesting a return to their suite when Quay pulled back.

"What do you need the milk for? Cereal?"

"Just to drink," her voice was as soft as her smile. She watched him find the milk and a glass and then she contented herself by watching new snow falling outside the windows in the alcove.

Laughter arrived a few moments later with Smoak, Sabra, Yohan and Melina.

"What's so funny?" Ty called from her chair.

"Yohan asked when Smoak and Sabra were gonna set a wedding date," Mel's violet house shoes slapped the polished hardwoods as she crossed over to the kitchen island.

"The groom says, 'when everything calms down'", Yohan shared, joining in when a yelp of laughter came from Quay's direction.

"Yeah, I'd say we can expect to hear something in about fifty years." Yohan added through his own laughter.

Sabra was clearly more at ease that morning. She nudged her softer shoulder against Yohan's harder more massive one. "It won't be that long," she made the promise while smoothing her hands across the seat of her yellow Yoga pants. "We at least have to wait 'til after your parent's wedding." She hopped into a vacant bar chair having referred to Josephine Ramsey's upcoming nuptials to her old flame and Yohan's biological father Crane Cannon.

"Isn't Dena supposed to be handling the event?"

"Sabra…" Smoak warned, not buying the innocence in his fiancée's query for a second.

"Alright…so what's on tap for the day?" She asked after sulking for a moment.

"The place is huge," Yohan went over to peer across the frost covered grounds from the patio doors at the rear of the kitchen. "Me and Meli are gonna walk around, check it out." He said.

"Well we've got access to all the vehicles." Ty announced. "There're even snow mobiles if the place is too much for walking."

"That sounds like fun." Mel exchanged a nod with her husband.

"Doesn't it?" Ty twirled her fingers around a tendril of hair that had fallen from her messy ponytail. "I'm gonna have to make a trip back here after the babies."

"Please," Sabra snorted. "Sorry to have to tell you this, girl, but Quay is gonna be as stupidly overprotective *after* the babies as he is now."

"Damn right," Quay went over to hand Ty a blue linen napkin to keep across her lap while she drank her milk.

The DeBurghs were next to arrive along with Taurus and Nile. Darby was like a kid when she raced over to the alcove and marveled at the snow.

"Girl, aren't you sick of snow livin' up in the Highlands?" Sabra reached for the coffee decanter while shaking her head amusedly.

Darby smiled at Sabra's mention of Scotland where she and Kraven resided. "Guess I spent so much time in Cali, I still haven't gotten my fill of *real* winters."

"Want to come exploring with me and Yohan?" Melina offered.

"Oooh that sounds like fun!" Darby clasped her hands.

Melina nodded just as excitedly. "Ty says they've got snow mobiles and everything."

"Forget it," Kraven told his wife.

Quay's bellowing laughter rang out. "Now Sabra, what were you saying about *me* being overprotective?"

"Kraven they're very safe," Ty reassured, setting her glass to the coffee table. "I had the chance to ride them when I've visited for my meetings."

"Were you pregnant then?"

"Yeah," Ty confirmed Kraven's query before she actually meant to. "It was during one of my last visits," she explained to Quay feeling his coal-colored stare boring into her.

"Right after I found out I was pregnant really. As you can see," she swept a hand along her body, "all is well." She looked back to Kraven. "Darby'll be fine."

"Right," Kraven graced Tykira with a soft smile and then looked to his elated wife. "Forget it." He said without an ounce of remorse.

"So what else is in store for the trip?" Nile asked while helping herself to a mug of the piping hot French roast coffee that practically crooned to her.

"Lots…" Ty sighed and rested her elbow along the back of her chair. "I hope that certain worry warts won't frown on the ice cruise we're set to take in a couple of days."

"That sounds like fun." Darby's tone was forlorn and she fixed her husband with a pouting look.

Kraven was taking the coffee pot from Nile. "What kind of boat are we taking?" He asked Ty.

"A yacht, I think." Ty fiddled with her robe's belt. "I don't know boats that well, but it's docked. You can feel free to check it out."

The wink Kraven slanted to Darby was enough to return her to her earlier giddy self. "So is the staff gonna put up a tree for us? I hadn't noticed one." Her emerald eyes shifted briefly around the kitchen.

"Oh, I almost forgot to tell you guys," Ty sat up straighter in the chair, her dark oval face appearing more animated. "The lodge likes to be as non-intrusive as possible. The staff can handle a tree for us or we can do it ourselves. We can have our pick of any tree we'd like to chop down and bring in. Decorations are in the closet off the main room."

"Whoo hoo! When do we set out?"

"You're not chopping down a bloody tree, Lass!" Kraven almost slammed down his mug.

"Jeez…" Sabra groaned.

"Well, well, we see everyone's up and at 'em!" Johari noted when she and Moses arrived with Pike and Belle.

"We're gonna have to put Kraven and Quay on bed rest if they don't stop worrying over their wives."

"So who's up for getting a Christmas tree?" Darby asked.

"Oh that sounds like fun," Belle took a chair next to Taurus and reached for the hazelnut blend that had brewed alongside the French Roast. "We could have a decorating party."

"Yeah…" Johari's eyes sparkled as merrily as her reddish brown mane presently bound into a loose ball atop her head. "That *does* sound like fun."

"Quite fun. There's just the little matter of find the tree and chopping it down." Kraven's voice was dry.

"Well that's why we have all these strapping males around the place." Ty said.

"Oh?" Sabra's brows rose. "Is *that* why?" her fake confusion drew laughter from the other girls.

The guys weren't as amused. Tree chopping was not exactly what they had in mind for how they wanted to spend a romantic getaway with their women.

Darby clapped and posted up on the toes of her house sandals. The movement sent her honey wheat curls bobbing. "So who gets to go?"

Kraven smiled. "As you can see we're all chomping at the bit to get out there, love."

Darby simply waved off her husband's pessimism. Reaching across the island, she grabbed one of the big coffee mugs. "We'll draw names. Four strapping males should be enough." She exchanged a wink with Tykira.

Moses abruptly cleared his throat. "Since me and Pike weren't here when all this talk started, we should be exempt from the drawing."

Pike raised his hand. "I second that."

"Come on y'all," Melina groaned. "It's only fair that *all* the guys go in the pot."

"I second that." Sabra said.

A ripple of hushed curses filtered the environment as names were placed on strips of paper pulled from the message pad that Sabella had taken from the counter.

Fernando and Contessa walked in with a yawning Quest in tow just as the last names were tossed into the deep red ceramic mug.

"What's with the long faces?" Fernando asked.

"Oh yaay," Taurus' deep voice was monotone. "You're just in time to find out who gets tree cutting duty."

"Don't ask for more clarification," Pike warned, his handsome face a picture of gloom. "It'll only confuse and anger you," he predicted.

Fernando and Quest traded shrugs and went about finding their breakfast. In the end, the four 'lucky' tree cutters were selected. Unenthused, Yohan, Pike, Kraven and Fernando agreed to set out after lunch to choose the tree. Gradually, folks made their breakfast choices and then headed off to varying areas of the house to enjoy their meals.

Tykira begged off anything more filling just then. The milk had been all she'd craved for the time being. She, Quay and Quest were last to leave the kitchen having taken more time to enjoy the snow which had been falling steady since the wee hours of the morning. When Ty was ready to leave, she started to push out of her chair, but winced and resumed her seating.

"Okay...okay..." she drawled.

"What?" Immediately alert, Quay was by her side. "What's wrong?"

Ty was laughing quietly. "Looks like our girls are gonna be big snow fans. I don't think they're ready to leave yet," she took Quay's hands and put one to either side of her belly that protruded quite nicely at five months of pregnancy.

Ty winced again just as Quay laughed. He was surprised by the double kicks he felt at the center of his palms.

"Isn't it too early for them to be moving around like that?" He asked.

"Guess not," she was laughing breathlessly by then. "Come over here Quest." She called to her brother-in-law.

Quest was standing to leave and give the couple their privacy.

Quaysar grinned. "I'm giving you permission to touch my wife," he inclined his head sharply. "Get over here."

Quest didn't require much prodding. The moment he put his hands in place over Ty's stomach, his nieces applied simultaneous kicks.

"Jeez they're in sync," he marveled with a hushed laugh. "Wonder if we were like that?" he asked his twin.

"We'll have to ask Ma," Quay smiled anew while thinking of Catrina Ramsey.

Last to arrive in the kitchen that morning, was Michaela. She'd decided to sleep in that day. The sounds of laughter and soft conversation had touched her ears before she actually set foot in the kitchen.

A genuine smile curved her mouth until she spotted the scene across the room. It was a beautiful scene; she'd never dispute that, but something about it prevented her from moving closer to take part in the joy of it.

Quiet as she'd come, Mick backed out of the kitchen. Quest looked up in time to catch a glimpse of his wife's departure.

CHAPTER FOUR

After breakfast, Sabella returned to her and Pike's suite for a change of shoes and a jacket. She'd planned to join Yohan and Melina for their snowy walk, but got sidetracked when she passed in front of the full length mirror near the walk in closet.

She smiled, gazing with love sparkling in her almond brown eyes at the baby bump that was slowly growing. She rubbed her hands across the swell and sent up a silent, thankful prayer for the chance she thought was lost to her and her husband forever.

As content as she felt though, the feeling was overshadowed. Soon, she was looking beyond the treasured 'bump' and on to the new plumpness she was noticing. Belle was certain she was- and would be- the only one who noticed. For a while, anyway…that didn't seem to make her feel any better.

Blinking then, she sensed his presence before she even looked around and saw him leaning on the doorframe of their bedroom suite. Hastily, she donned an auburn colored scarf.

"Going to explore with Yohan and Mel," she was reaching for the burnt umber cashmere jacket when his arm encircled her waist.

Pike nuzzled his darkly bronzed face into Belle's neck and breathed in. "You have to go right now?" his baritone voice was a murmur.

"I told them I would…" her voice failed her when his hands cradled her breasts outlined against the square bodice of the sandy brown sweater she wore.

"What was that?" The query told her that he knew how affected by him she was. His thumbs had already gone to work on assaulting her nipples until they stood as erect nubs. He brought his mouth to her ear and suckled the lobe with a subtlety that made her pant.

Belle had intended her moan to be more of a refusal or at the very least a request that they save the interlude for a later time. Refusals would have to wait; he had her jaw in hand, angling her head for his kiss.

She put her all into the kiss, thrusting her tongue against his with an intense desperation. How else was she to have responded? She rarely- she *never* refused him. When his fingers curled into the waistband of her black Yoga pants, she somehow found the ability to do precisely that.

"Isak I really do want to get some fresh air," her voice was hushed as she slipped out of his embrace. She put a quick peck to his mouth, careful not to make eye contact and left the room.

***

Michaela; needing to work off some of the unexpected stress she'd encountered, found a dance partner in Darby. The two located a rec room with space and a sound system to rival Sabra's dance studios at her Vegas resort.

"You better not let Sabra hear you say that!" Darby chided while doing a few knee bends in preparation for the workout.

They'd found a dock to set up Mick's IPOD and soon after, they were grooving like the great dancers they were. With En Vogue's "*My Lovin' (Never Gonna Get It)*" pulsing throughout the room, the women moved around intermittently falling into sync atop the gleaming oak floors in the glass enclosed room. With the splendid wintry scene visible from the insulated floor to ceiling windows all around, laughter flooded into the music. The sensation of freedom and giddiness overflowed.

The volume of laughter took precedence when the En Vogue single faded seconds before the Prince classic *"Erotic City"* began. Still energized, Michaela and Darby continued to bounce around the room much to the satisfaction of their husbands. The men had gone looking for their wives and made the happy discovery within minutes of each other.

Unbeknownst to Darby and Mick, Kraven and Quest shared matching armchairs in the viewing area above the studio. With their legs propped on the Ottomans before the chairs, the guys indulged in the show. They held not an ounce of guilt over the idea that they may have been infringing on their wives' privacy.

"This is such a great vacation," Kraven's sing song voice was a matter-of-fact monotone. His vivid shamrock gaze was riveted on Darby.

"Best ever," Quest agreed in the same intent manner. His hypnotic gray eyes hadn't shifted from Mick since he'd settled into the chair.

"I'd much rather be doing *this* instead of chopping down some bloody tree."

Quest chuckled. "If you don't do it, Darby will."

"God you're right," Kraven laughed as his head fell back a little. "The woman will probably not settle down 'til she's in labor."

"You're a lucky man."

"As are you, mate." Kraven smiled thoughtfully. "Quincee's an angel."

"This I know," Quest sighed the words, his hazy stare turning even softer as the image of his little girl filled his mind. Just as suddenly, another thought emerged and brought shadow to his face.

"I don't want her to be alone in the world, Kray."

"I don't see how that can happen!" Kraven's laughter was a bit wicked. "Quay and Ty are providing her with a house full of playmates."

"It's just that Mick grew up so lonely." Quest shared once laughter over his twin and sister-in-law had subsided. "She never thought she could trust anybody. Sometimes, I still think she feels that way." Quest withdrew a little watching Mick dancing around to the sounds of a Jody Watley tune then.

"I just don't want Quinn growing up that way, you know?"

Kraven nodded, having turned to give Quest the benefit of his gaze. "I'd say Mick turned out just fine, despite all that." He crossed one flip-flop shod foot over the other and slid down further in his chair.

The Jody Watley classic faded into another vintage piece. Kraven and Quest carried on their conversation while The Dazz Band's *"Let It Whip"*, rumbled through the speakers.

"I don't think she wants another baby."

Kraven's gaze reflected deeper understanding then. "So is this about Quinn being lonely or you wanting to make another angel with your beautiful wife?"

"Right..." Kraven said when Quest offered up no answer. "I understand that very well, man. If I have my way, Darby's gonna give me a crew to rival Quay's."

Soft male chuckling warmed the atmosphere. Soon, the guys had returned their attention to the lovely visions on the dance floor.
***

Despite all reluctance, the tree cutters remained true to their responsibilities. They headed off just after lunch to locate the perfect specimen. They were returning in just over an hour.

Tykira evidently approved their efforts. She applauded when the foursome arrived with a wide and towering pine tree.

"No one should have a complaint about this," she raved, looking way up at what had to be an eleven or twelve footer.

"They can shove this tree up their ass if they do." Yohan muttered.

"Bet you won't say that to Mel," Ty challenged, folding her arms over the front of her azure overalls.

Yohan gave Tykira's ponytail a playful tug. "How about we keep my point of view among the five of us?"

Ty giggled. "I second that."

Kraven groaned while he and Fernando worked excess branches from the base of the tree. "I say we shut off all voting for the duration of the trip."

"I second that." Pike grumbled.

The guys went about their business, trying to decide on the best place to set the tree in the main room. While they debated, Ty helped out by collecting the few pine cones that had fallen from the tree as the guys brought it inside. She collected the cones and arranged them around the large, elegantly designed room. The cones proved to be wonderful decorative additions. She was on her knees then, reaching for a cone that had rolled beneath an end table.

"What the fuck, Ty?! Dammit! What the hell are you guys doin' lettin' her crawl around on the floor like this?!"

Yohan, Pike, Kraven and Fernando had all whirled around at Quay's outburst. They forgot all about the tree. When an exaggerated silence covered the room, it was the sound of the tree falling over that punctuated Quay's bellow.

The agitated father-to-be helped his wife to her feet. Then, he fixed the other men in the room with glares before turning back to Tykira.

Ty; thoroughly outraged at her husband by then, refused his help when he would have carried her from the room. She slapped at his arms, pushed him aside and then stalked out ahead of him.

The brush off did nothing to soothe Quay's temper. He cast another glare at the four men before leaving after his wife.

"Yikes," Yohan rolled his eyes once his cousin vacated the room. "How about y'all keep your distance when Belle and Darby get further along?" He urged Kraven and Pike.

"I second that," Fernando added.

CHAPTER FIVE

A skeptical look had taken hold of Johari's expression as she stirred her virgin daiquiri. "We aren't going for the element of surprise here, are we?" She asked.

Sabella laughed over the word. "Surprise? My cousin's one of the guests of honor."

"Right." Johari shook a finger in the air.

Before dusk, the group began to collect in the main room to get the tree decorating underway. Sabra assisted, or rather took over, the job of decided which ornaments to select from among the resort staff's provisions.

The rest of the ladies used the time to lightly toss about ideas for an intimate engagement party.

"Do we need to make trips into town for gifts?" County asked.

Melina was already shaking her head. "Shouldn't be necessary since we'll do that at whatever big soirée Georgia gives them."

"Hmph," Mick massaged the bridge of her nose, "and we definitely don't want her thinking we've overstepped."

Belle laughed again, resituating herself on the loveseat she shared with Ty. "The fact that we're even *discussing* a party is overstepping in Aunt Georgia's eyes."

"So the trick is to do something as far removed from anything Georgia would come up with." Nile suggested.

Darby snapped her fingers which were half hidden beneath the oversized cuffs of her caramel colored knit sweater. "Maybe we could get the staff to help us set up a winter barbeque our last night here?"

"Oh that sounds perfect," Ty clasped her hands and gave them a triumphant shake. "I'll talk to the staff tomorrow."

Mick served up a sly smile. "Are you sure your husband won't think *talking* is too much for you in your condition?"

Everyone, including Ty laughed over the playful barb directed at Quay.

"He's about to drive me half crazy," Ty confessed once some of the laughter had settled.

"Fernando said Quay was the one who looked half crazy when he walked up in here today and saw you crawling around looking for pine cones." County snorted a laugh that was contagious.

"He's just concerned," Johari finally called out over the laughter. "Rightfully so, since you're getting further along."

Ty shook her head. "At the rate we're going, he'll think the labor's too much exertion and forbid me to deliver the babies."

"Here, here," Mick cheered and lead everyone to raise their glasses in toast to Quaysar Ramsey.

~~~

"Stop bein' a wimp. It's not like you're drivin' or anything." Sabra showed off her bartending skills later that night.

Half the decorating was done. All that remained was to rope the last string of lights around the tree and turn it on.

"I'll pass," Johari eyed the drink that appeared equal parts vodka, gin and scotch along with other ingredients she wouldn't chance a guess at. "I drink that and I won't be able to make it up the stairs, let alone drive a car."

"Shit Jo, is Moses ordering you not to drink or somethin'?"

Johari easily excused Sabra's unfiltered manner and simply raised her glass. "Me and my daiquiri-"

"Virgin," Sabra interjected.

"Are just fine," Johari took the fresh pitcher she'd prepared and left the bar. She never saw her husband who had kept his distance but stood close enough to overhear the exchange.

"Are you as big a wimp as your wife?" Sabra called when she saw her cousin.

Moses' playful dangerous grin emerged and he strolled closer to the bar. "Hit me," he told her.

~~~

Kraven's thoughtful observation of his wife hadn't stopped at the risqué dance performance she'd taken part in with Mick earlier that day. Something about her behavior had him curious. He wasn't sure there was anything wrong, but something was definitely... off.

He watched her flitting from place to place. She took part in almost every conversation in the room for all of a minute before she was off to see to something else. He caught up to her seconds after she'd milled about at the bar with County and Sabra for a few moments.

Darby hugged him tight, elated and out of breath. "Isn't this so much fun?"

Kraven cupped her face and captured her green stare with his own. "What's the matter with you?"

"What?" She pulled down his hands.

Kraven turned the tables and imprisoned her hands against his chest. "What's with all this energy?"

"I'm just happy is all," she focused on where her fingers toyed with one of the buttons on the wheat colored shirt he wore outside a pair of coffee brown trousers. "I don't think I have any more energy than usual." She shrugged.

"Can't say I agree with that," he looked with interest toward her breasts pressing against where her hands lay on his chest. "Quest and I caught yours and Michaela's...workout this morning."

Darby's uncommon gaze narrowed playfully. "Perverts," she curved into him a bit more snuggly.

Kraven raised one broad shoulder in a shrug. "Sue me."

"Hmm..." she pretended to consider that. "I can think of something a lot more fun to do with you than that." With those words, she pulled his dark head down to meet her kiss.

~~~

Belle poured a cup of fresh brewed blueberry tea yet hesitated before reaching for the honey to sweeten it. She sensed her husband near and smiled when he made his presence known.

"When are you planning to eat?" He asked.

"Been eating all day," she grimaced, "Can't you tell?" She murmured too low for him to hear.

Pike waited for her to proffer a more appropriate reply to his question.

Sabella went about adding the honey yet rolled her eyes when Pike took a seat along the edge of the heavy, food laden buffet table. Arms folded across a loose fitting hunter green sweater, he watched her even more closely.

"I'll eat when I'm hungry, Isak."

"Will you?"

"Why are you making a big deal of this?" She slammed the honey jar to the table but managed to keep her voice controlled. "We're supposed to be having fun."

"Agreed. But let's not forget that you're the same woman who was practically starving herself a few months ago."

The reminder hurt and it showed. At once, Pike regretted voicing it.

"I'm sorry Bella. I just need to know you're okay."

She moved close then to take his face in her hands. She enjoyed a few moments of studying his remarkable burnished gold features.

"I'm okay Isak, I promise. Please don't go crazy on me."

His smile hinged on faint laughter. "That a dig at your cousin?"

Belle lowered her hands to curve her fingers into the slight V neck of his sweater. "We don't need *two* crazy dads roaming the place, you know?"

Pike nodded, conceding her point. Then, his expression sobered and he brushed the back of his hand across her forehead and cheek. "Sure you're okay?"

"I'm sure."

He jerked her into a sudden, starved kiss that had Belle moaning her pleasure after only a few heated thrusts of his tongue. Nevertheless, those nagging strains of unease wormed their way into the moment. Delicately, so as not to stir his curiosity, she eased herself out of the kiss by initiating a series of soft pecks to his lips as she progressive withdrew.

"Promised I'd help check the tree lights," she kissed his cheek and then took her tea and left.

Belle's attempt to not stroke her husband's curiosity hadn't worked. As usual, his instincts were spot on. His dark eyes were concern and suspicion filled as he watched her go.

***

"If you hang up this phone Lee, I swear-"

"What? You'll fire me? Good luck running this place from the wilderness because the second you give me my walking papers I'm *runnin'* the hell out of here."

Sabra closed her eyes in reference to her general manager's 'wilderness' reference. The wireless connection definitely wasn't the best given the weather conditions. Steadily falling snow had dropped the temperatures along with the phone service.

Following a late night of tree decorating and making merry, she and Smoak returned to their suite. Of course they didn't drift into sleep until two hours later.

She still ached in the most delicious way when she eased out of bed, stole her fiancé's phone and contacted Lee Lee Arnold. So as not to risk waking Smoak, Sabra kept the lights off and crept into the bathroom to use the phone. At 5am it was still dark yet Sabra knew the office was coming back to life in Vegas.

"I just want to make sure everything's okay. There were some fires burning when I left-"

"And I'm not telling you whether they're flamin' like hell or about to go out."

"Damn you-"

"Now, now no need for all that. Just go on and fire me. I could use the break."

"Smoak put you up to this, didn't he? Told you not to tell me anything?"

"Enjoy your vacation, girl." With that, Lee Lee hung up.

Not quite believing the call had ended so abruptly, Sabra gave the phone a shake. "Lee?" She hissed and then slammed the phone to the counter at the realization that the woman had hung up on her.

Sabra turned to lean on the counter and gasped. She saw Smoak's silhouette outlined in the moonlight streaming past the bathroom window. Beautifully naked and relaxing against the doorframe, he kept his arms folded over a broad licorice dark chest while he watched her.

"I was just checking the weather," Sabra coolly delivered the lie she'd selected in case he caught her with the phone.

Smoak left the doorframe and went to peer out of the window. "Still snowing." He announced. "How's Lee Lee?"

"Damn you," she blurted. "You can't just expect me to forget all about work."

He'd moved close and was propping her chin to his fist. "I love it that you can't forget all about your work." His thumb began a slow stroke of her bottom lip. "It's your job to take care of your business and it's my job to take care of you." He nudged her chin with his fist then. "I take my job very seriously." He whispered.

She swallowed when he stepped between her legs. The width of his unyielding frame made her open wide to him. She could feel cool air brush her heated intimate folds when the short, ice blue silk robe gaped.

Smoak wasn't altogether pleased to find her clothed, as lovely as the garment was.

"So what does your job involve?" Her voice was breathy as he roughly tugged her out of the robe.

"I'm on the servicing end."

"I see," her heart was in her throat. "And which uh…end do you prefer?"

"Hard to have a preference when there're so many good ones to choose from." The robe was properly dismissed to the floor and he took her in one rigid, plundering stroke the moment his words silenced.

Sabra would have let her head fall back, but he'd taken a fistful of her hair and prevented any movement. Smoak demanded her kiss without speaking a word and she eagerly obeyed, crying out when he suddenly withdrew his body from hers.

He turned her to face the sink and took her from behind once she was bent over the counter to his satisfaction. Again, one hand fisted her thick hair while his mouth ravaged her neck. He alternated between the satiny dark chocolate column and the sensitive spot below her earlobe.

His free hand clutched her hip and then eased down to finger her clit. All the while his thick, licorice toned erection lunged in and out of the ever-moistening walls of her sex.

"Shut up," he ordered quietly when her cries gained volume. He gave her hair a bit of a warning jerk.

"Okay, okay..." she gasped and moaned intermittently.

The obedient tone she used- so terribly uncharacteristic of her- rendered Smoak unable to hold out against her. In seconds, he was spewing the proof of his need inside her. Sabra came soon after just as his hands rose up to weigh her breasts. His thumbs flicked the nipples, driving her pleasure into another gear.

For long moments after, they remained curved over the counter in an awkward yet deliciously satisfying embrace.

CHAPTER SIX

"Damn…"

"Complaints? Should I do *this* instead?"

A low rumble started deep inside the massive molasses dark wall that was Yohan Ramsey's chest when Melina switched the clockwise rotations of her hips to a counter clockwise movement. She bit down on her lip as sensation permeated her entire body. She expelled a wavery moan and stilled herself to savor the moment.

Yohan was having none of that. His wide hands practically smothered her hips when he took them and moved her up and down his throbbing shaft.

"Fuck…" he groaned, squeezing his alluring deep set eyes completely shut. "That's it… damn Meli…that's it…"

Melina drew her fingers through her thick hair and gave herself over to Yohan's handling of her body. She cried out when he stiffened in the tell-tale sign that prefaced him coming. Moments later, the warmth of his seed was coating the walls of her sex.

Once the aftershocks of their mutual fulfillment began to ebb, Yohan let Melina drift down to rest on top of him. She smiled, her lashes drifting shut over her eyes as she relished her husband's closeness.

"Good morning," she whispered.

"Morning," he smirked, "sorry I didn't get around to saying that before."

"You had a lot on your mind."

"I still do," Yohan flipped her over beneath him. "A thing like that can drive a man crazy."

"Well we can't have that," she giggled, "*one* crazy acting Ramsey around here is enough."

Yohan hid his very dark, very gorgeous face in his wife's neck. He chuckled over the mention of his cousin and the previous day's outburst. "If we do something like this next Christmas, I vote for leaving all expectant fathers at home."

Melina felt her heart flip and she knew it wasn't wholly due to Yohan's mouth blazing a path across the rise of her bosom.

"You think you'd be like that?"

"Like what?" His response carried on an absent chord.

"If you were an expectant father?"

Again, Yohan chuckled. He shifted his weight from Mel to rest on his side. "Given who my role model for fatherhood is, I try not to think too much about what I'd be like. *Too* much?" He muttered something obscene. "I don't think about it at all."

"So you'd really let Marcus deprive you of something like that?" She trailed her index nail about the broad ridge of his bicep.

"It's not about what I'd *let* happen, Meli. It's about what already is." He pounced on her then as though newly ravenous.

Melina; caught between exquisite pleasure and stinging sorrow, ordered herself to calm.
***

As was customary every morning, Taurus reached for his wife. After catching her and drawing her close, kisses and intense fondling were followed by a lengthy bout of lovemaking. Their very active sex life, gave Nile all the inspiration she needed to create more of the beautifully erotic artwork she was known for. It went without saying that Taurus was equally inspired.

It also went without saying that everyone who knew him believed Taurus Ramsey was a new man since he'd reclaimed the woman he loved.

When Taurus reached for Nile that morning, however, things didn't go according to their usual plan. A subtle frown marred the flawless area between his long, amber colored brows. Gradually, he forced open his eyes to prove to himself that she wasn't there next to him.

He didn't have long to hunt. She was on the window seat in the alcove and surrounded by bright wrapping paper. Ribbons littered the carpet and the tops of her bare feet.

"Getting your Christmas presents wrapped sort of early, huh?" Taurus asked once he'd pushed himself up against the pillow lined headboard.

"Le bon bébé de Matin," Nile greeted her husband good morning in her native tongue and blew him a kiss. "This is for Tykira," she explained.

"Why?" Taurus queried through a yawn.

"Bête…" Nile sighed that he was silly. "She's pregnant with your little cousins- it's the gift for her shower."

Grinning, Taurus pulled a hand through the thick waves of his light brown hair. "You think Quay'll let the girl open 'em? Job might be too much for her to handle."

"Stop," Nile softly chastised. "You all should go easier on Quay. He's got every right to be concerned. Ty's carrying *two* babies." She smiled reflectively while pressing clear tape to the side of the box. She was about to add a bow when she was pulled to her feet.

"Taurus-"

"Come back to bed."

"I will, douceur," *Sweetness* she'd called him and patted his cheek. "I'm almost done."

"Now," he insisted, giving her ear a coaxing nuzzle while fondling her beneath the sheer turquoise robe she wore.

"I really want to get this done, love." She moaned.

"Is the shower tonight?" His tongue thrust into her ear, mimicking the way his middle finger pleasured her then.

"Mmm…no…"

"Then come back to bed," easily he lifted her against him, plunging his tongue slow and deep inside her mouth.

Nile figured the gift wrapping could hold for a while longer.

***

Contessa resituated her palm on the plum comforter. That time, she grabbed a fistful of the satiny covering. Her improved position, allowed her to meet her husband's fire with more of her own.

Fernando rested his forehead against her honey-toned shoulder. He moaned in such a way that County felt a shiver of triumph over her power to affect him so. That morning, the newlyweds began their day with a naughty session in the bedroom that was still dimmed thanks to heavy unopened plum draperies.

County planted a fist in the pillow nearest her, biting down harder on her lip with every lunge he made into her from behind.

The firm mattress dipped beneath them when Fernando added his other knee to the bed. He took County's hips in both hands, keeping her steady for the thrusts that moved with greater speed-greater depth. Hunching over her then, his hands smoothed up along her side and curved around to cradle one wildly bouncing breast.

County's whimpering moan stroked her husband's cocky arrogance then. Intent on driving her even crazier, he brushed his thumb across the bud and turned the tanned nipple into a conductor for the ribbons of sensation sprouting through her with renewed intensity.

"Quiet down," he growled against the hair tapered at her nape when her moans turned into shrieks.

To punish her for the outburst, Fernando planted a slap to the side of one buttock before smoothing over the area and grabbing it for a quick tug.

Contessa expected her heart to beat right out of her throat- the pounding was just that potent. She had no idea where she was stealing all her energy.

Fernando had been insatiable since their arrival at the lodge- more insatiable than usual anyway and that was saying a lot. The bedroom had seen an abundance of action as did the bathroom and more than a few of the closets throughout the large house.

To smother a sudden desire to scream her pleasure, County buried her face in one of the pillows that was strewn across the four poster queen bed. The position increased penetration tenfold and soon it was Fernando smothering a groan into his wife's shoulder as deep shudders wracked his powerful frame when release hit him.

Deliciously spent, Fernando collapsed atop her. Soon after, County gave way beneath his crushing weight to lay flat on her tummy beneath him.

"Am I wearing you out?"

The question was a growl into her shoulder. County's mouth tilted upward into a lazy smile. "Yes you are and thank you." She slurred. "Ramsey?"

"Hmm…"

"You weigh a ton."

Chuckling, Fernando eased off and turned County to her back. "Better?" He settled himself over her again.

He was still crushing her, but the renewed sense of pleasure spiraling through her made the 'crush' quite delightful.

Fernando grazed a pair of gorgeously shaped lips down Contessa's neck and across her chest.

"We're gonna make our duo a threesome if we keep this up," he murmured.

When he lifted his head to stare down at her, County didn't have time to mask the sudden unease that flashed in her brown eyes.

"You okay?" A frown had drawn his sleek brows close.

"Threesome? Aren't I enough woman for you?" She purposefully led him to believe she'd misunderstood.

Fernando grinned, his adorable eye crinkle returning. "Where'd you get such a dirty mind?"

"Haven't you met my cousins?"

He nodded over the memory and then sobered somewhat and placed his hand on her belly. Adding the slightest pressure, his thumb grazed her navel.

"Three," he said.

County couldn't pretend to misunderstand that time. She offered no response, but took his hand and urged it down over the bare triangle above her sex. Her lashes fluttered the moment his fingers brushed her intimate petals still moistened from their earlier activities.

She bit her lip again and commenced a subtle grind of her hips atop the tangled bed coverings. Fernando; having had his train of thought regarding family detoured, let his face fall back into the crook of County's neck. His fingers soaked in her ever mounting juices.

Soon after, the newlyweds were in the depths of another intimate scene.

***

Later that morning, Sabra and Sabella enjoyed hot creamy cocoa. They were curled up in matching, white cushioned oak framed chairs that furnished the patio and balconies of the lodge.

Sabra; who's cocoa contained more than the usual ingredients, blew across the surface of the rich liquid in her oversized mug. She inhaled the aroma of chocolate and rum filling her nostrils.

"You've said some dumb things in your life, but this is one of the dumbest." Sabra scolded once she'd sipped and savored a swig of the cocoa.

"Drinking a bit more lately, aren't we?" Belle noted.

"I'm happy," Sabra excused, turning serious in an instant. "Smoak knows everything I never wanted him to know and he still loves me…I feel like I can handle anything." She toasted with her mug. "Even a little drink during the holidays."

"Hmph," Belle sniffed, though inwardly she was elated by her cousin's contentment.

"And don't change the subject," Sabra scolded again. "Doubting Pike should be the last thing you *ever* do."

"I'm not doubting him," Belle wrapped herself tighter in the heavy silver blue blanket she'd brought along.

"How can that be if you think he'll leave you if you get fat?"

"Jesus Sabi…you never listen." Belle rolled her eyes.

"So explain it to me," Sabra enjoyed another sip of the cocoa. "Explain it so I'll understand."

Belle sipped her 'virgin' cocoa then. "Isak always loved me," she smiled at the thought of her husband. "Back then…I didn't know what he saw in me…but he saw it and he never let go of it."

"Right," Sabra tucked her jean clad legs beneath her. "He loved you before you had my little cousin in there to blame for your luscious thickness." She shifted Belle a condescending frown. "You really are stupid, you know?"

"You can't understand, Sabi. You've never worried about your weight."

"Hey! I'm no weed!"

"But you've never stressed over *not* being a weed."

"What the hell for?" Sabra set aside her mug and spread her arms wide. "Girl, women would *kill* to be able to flaunt what we have. You've pulled a god like Isak Tesano and you *still* don't recognize your own power. My guess is he wants you more now *because* his baby's inside you-men are weird like that…" She shrugged.

"Good luck with givin' him the brush off because you're suddenly pressed about adding a few pounds," Sabra reached for her mug again. "I seriously doubt he'll let you get away with *that* again."

CHAPTER SEVEN

Darby plopped herself onto Kraven's lap, sitting astride him while he leaned back on the bed's cushioned headboard. She smoothed the back of her hand across his arms which were folded across his expansive sun-kissed chest.

"What's wrong?" She asked.

"You first," he countered, resting his head back on the padded board to watch her more easily beneath his hooded gaze. "I know it's something and since I tried to get it out of you when we were decorating that bloody tree, I think I'm entitled to have my answer first."

Darby lowered her eyes to study a pear-shaped scar embedded along one side of his chiseled eight pack of abs. "So I guess you're not buying that I'm overly giddy because it's Christmas and-" she waved wildly. "It's snowing, man!" She motioned toward the beige draperies. They were parted to reveal the windows and flakes of white that bumped the glass and stuck to it.

"So you're happy because it's snowing?" He smiled, lazily sliding his gaze toward the shower of white beyond the window.

"Doesn't that make sense?"

"It does, but this is *you* we're talking about."

Again she looked down, studying the path her fingers made as they grazed the ripple of muscle that packed his beautifully cut abs.

Kraven posted his fist beneath her chin and nudged until she looked at him. "You've got to see it by now, how well I know you. While a snowy Christmas is an awesome thing, I think we both know it's about more than that, don't we?"

He moved his fist to cup her cheek. "You're happy, Lass. That's quite obvious. So am I. I feel like I could burst from it but in you I sense nervousness. I'm right, aren't I?"

At last, Darby nodded. "I never thought I'd be a mom. I never even planned on it." She spread her arms and gave a little shimmy. "I was Nile Becquois' sexy PR person, living footloose and fancy free in Cali and I loved it."

Kraven's smile narrowed his brilliant gaze. He adored the way her curls bounced around her lovely honey brown face. She'd slipped into a nightshirt, but had left the simple black linen garment unbuttoned. For a time, Kraven gazed with interest at how the shirt gaped open to reveal the alluring swells of her abundant bosom.

"Now I'm gonna be a mom," she was saying, "and I love that too," she looked at him, "but it scares me. It scares the hell out of me. My mom was so great at this," she smirked. "I didn't always appreciate how great she was but uh…" She winced playfully. "She was pretty damn fantastic at it. Raising girls isn't easy and there were times when I was more than a handful."

"You? No…" Kraven drawled. For emphasis, he cupped his hands about her butt and squeezed until she laughed.

"I don't want to mess up," Darby confessed once she'd sobered a little. "The kid deserves the best."

"The kid already has the best." He growled the words while nibbling a spot along her jaw.

"Thank you," she sighed when he let her ease back. "Sorry for all the anxiety. Guess you didn't know what you were really getting into when you married me, huh?"

In response, Kraven tightened the hold he had on her derriere. In one enviably effortless move, he lifted her and eased her down to sheath his erection.

Darby's sharp cry muffled when she bit into her bottom lip. She moved then as though she'd suddenly been injected with some mind altering drug that triggered every one of her erogenous zones.

"I really know what I've gotten myself into," he followed her every movement, her every reaction as she took him.

Darby lifted her arms, tugging her hands through her hair which caused the sleep shirt to gape wider. Kraven raised a knee to angle her closer to his mouth. A massive thigh supported her back and he took the tip of one breast between his lips. Suckling lightly at first, he soon added his tongue to the play, gently circling it about a dusky brown nipple.

Darby opened her mouth to moan; but there was no sound forthcoming. She twirled her hips in a wicked, sensual dance clenching her walls about his wide shaft and arching more of her breast into his mouth.

Kraven granted the unspoken plea. He offered a sound of genuine male approval and sucked the nipple as though he were suddenly obsessed by the feel of it against his tongue.

She gasped his name, mingling it among naughty groans of satisfaction. Laying her palms flat on the thick layers of muscle that defined his chest, she worked her hips in a more frenzied manner. She was more than eager to reach the crest of ultimate satisfaction that she knew awaited with just a few additional strokes from his remarkable erection.

She was moist beyond reason. In the very quiet expanse of their bedroom suite, only the rustle of sheets and gentle slurping from her drenched sex could be heard as her walls massaged his breathtaking endowment.

***

Later that morning, the guests arrived for breakfast in a slow procession. Many appeared drowsy as though they craved more sleep or…more of what they'd been up to in the earliest hours which had increased the need for more down time.

The somewhat magical cook staff had been requested to provide the rations that morning. The guests' sleep sexy stares took in the smorgasbord of delectable breakfast entrees that were presented on a long wooden serving board table before a bay window in the dining area.

"So Ty, exactly what is an *ice cruise*?"

Tykira; already eating from her own loaded plate, paused. "Why? Does it sound weird?"

Moses patted Johari's hip. "Get some of those," he pointed toward the tea biscuits on a basket in the middle of the table. Then, he turned back to Ty. "No. I just never heard of one before."

"Sounds uncomfortable." Taurus said on his way to the fridge for juice.

"That's a nice way of putting it." Smoak yawned and took the pitcher of milk from the table.

"Y'all are a bunch of wimps," Sabra sniffed at the rich gravy that had been provided for the grits. "Scared to try somethin' new, so sad."

"Well do *you* know what an ice cruise is?" Quay asked. "Mmm hmm," he rolled his eyes when Sabra didn't respond.

Ty laughed around the bite of beef bacon she'd just taken. "Well I think Pike and Kraven already checked out our transportation." She looked toward the expectant fathers who nodded once in sync before turning back to fill their plates.

"So the cruise won't be on a ship but rather a yacht that's docked at the pier." She explained. "We'll set out around lunchtime on the man-made pond that surrounds the resort. It's temperature controlled, so we won't have to worry about it freezing. The yacht'll carry us into town for lunch or whatever else we might want to do and then we'll head back around dusk- that'll give us the chance to see the lights coming on."

"Gosh Ty that sounds beautiful," County said, pausing from smothering her French toast in maple syrup.

Tykira's serene smile lit up her lovely slightly rounded face. "The owners expect it to be one of their premiere attractions when the resort opens to the winter crowds next season."

"So what do we do until it's time to head out?" Mick asked from her spot at the end of the island.

"I've got a good idea," Yohan picked up a full plate in one hand and slung his wife across his shoulder. "Back to bed."

The kitchen erupted into laughter.

***

After downing her fill of a splendid breakfast, Mick was back in the suite and once again cursing the poor job she'd done with her packing. Birth control was the last thing she should be forgetting and especially on a trip like this.

She had managed-barely- to distract Quest with talk of all they'd uncovered about Dena and Jasper Stone aka Eston Perjas and the consequences still to come. Mick knew her husband very well though. He wouldn't be persuaded from his preferred course of action for much longer.

The room door slamming behind her didn't deter Mick from searching her bags.

"We need to talk."

The intensity of Quest's voice as it vibrated through the large room was what sent Mick turning to frown in his direction.

"Don't bother acting like you don't know what about." His hands disappeared inside the denim pockets hidden by the slate gray fleece hoody he wore.

"Why'd you leave the kitchen?"

"Well hell Quest, breakfast was over," she made a poor attempt at laughter. "I was gonna take a shower before we met everybody for the cruise."

The gradual rise of his temper reflected in the darkening of his stare. Quest took a slow appraisal of his wife's body- beginning at her red wine polished toes that peeked out from the hem of a white cotton robe. The appraisal travelled upward then over the bulky garment to observe her beckoning dark chocolate face and the onyx curls framing it.

"Why'd you leave the kitchen that day you saw me there with Quay and Ty?"

Guilt registered in her exquisite amber stare when she blinked. Quest regretted that he'd guessed correctly at her mood.

"You should start talking if you expect us to be on time for this cruise," he reached behind him to flip the lock on the bedroom door.

"I didn't want to interrupt you guys…"

"You're a better liar that that," his voice was quiet, cautionary.

She rolled her eyes and waved him off. "I didn't come on vacation to be cross examined." She turned to zip her suitcase shut.

Quest pushed off the door. "Seems like you didn't come on vacation to do a lot of things."

She rounded on him, "What's that supposed to mean?"

Quest didn't stop advancing until he was standing over his wife's petite frame. "Every time I come close, you come up with some way to take my mind off you."

"I have not!" Her eyes fired amber daggers then. When he inclined his head and smiled, she couldn't ignore the feeling her heart made when it flipped at the spark of his lone left dimple.

"Alright," his tone wasn't reassuring in the least. He reached around her and pushed the case to the floor. Then, he was unfastening the belt that secured her robe.

Before Mick realized it, she was doing what she'd so vehemently denied seconds before.

"We don't have time for this. We need to get ready for the cruise." Her lashes settled over her eyes the instant the words left her tongue.

Quest didn't call her on it. He finished with the belt. Once the robe fell open he took his time admiring the view she provided him. His eyes had gone pure black then from desire as opposed to loss of temper.

He tilted his head to follow the line his index finger trailed from the valley between her steadily heaving breasts and down her tummy. Then, he was brushing the back of his hand over the bare skin above her sex.

"Quest-"

He allowed her the fraction of time to speak his name before filling her mouth with his tongue.

There was no question that she wanted him. She always wanted him but there were consequences to playing with fire.

"Let's wait 'til we have more-more time…" she gave a valiant attempt at halting the mounting scene when he freed her mouth. Resistance fled her mind when he stopped brushing the back of his hand across her sensitized flesh and stroked her sex. The silken chocolate toned petals reacted to the faintest touch of his fingers. A sweet ache swelled, demanding to be soothed by him and him alone.

Wait, she mouthed the word yet it carried no volume. His tongue was in her mouth again and her response was instant and eager. The eagerness intensified when his middle finger invaded her depths, commencing a slow exploration. Five seconds hadn't passed before the tip of his finger was slick with her moisture.

Michaela scarcely took note of him lifting her and putting her on the bed in one fluid move. She would've grazed her nails through the silky, close cut waves of his hair but he took hold of her wrists and kept them above her head.

Mick's eyelids felt heavy against the pressure of her need and she was practically panting for him then. Quest took her mouth once more. He'd filled his free hand with one of her heaving breasts and proceeded to shamelessly molest the nipple into a firmer nub. He broke the kiss to suckle the nipple he'd assaulted, drawing the bud deeper into his mouth when she squirmed beneath him.

"Quest please...please...I-I'm asking you..."

Whether he misunderstood or merely pretended to, he didn't let on. Hungrily, he fed at her breast and at the same time returned his hand to her sex. Soft, ocean deep groans surged from his throat as he took more of her into his mouth. His fingers explored her ever more thoroughly and he took his time coaxing her to the threshold of climax.

In the end, he decided not to pull her all the way through that door with just a mere fingering to show for it. Instead, he unfastened his jeans, freed himself and took her before she'd come down off the high of her *almost* orgasm.

Mick clutched the front of his sweatshirt when his hold loosened on her wrists but refusal was no longer her intention. Slowly, she met his ravenous thrusts. She shuddered, wisps of breath escaping her parted lips. She tried to cry out when both his hands curved about her thighs, spreading them wider so he could take her deeper.

Quest brought his head down to hers. He outlined the shape of her lips with the tip of his nose. Next, he slipped his thumb inside and watched her suckle the digit and moan while her hips bucked more feverishly against his.

The sight of her working her X-rated mouth up and down the length of his thumb, sent his stiff chocolate-dipped, sex throbbing almost painfully as it plunged and stirred inside her. Michaela's hiccupping gasps close to his ear, inflamed his ego and Quest smiled at the pleasure it evoked.

Heavily, he came inside her. His grip firmed on her thighs when it seemed as if she were tensing against him. Selfishly, he kept her lush silken limbs spread to his approval until he was completely spent inside her. Even then, he remained sheathed amidst her core for a long while afterward.

CHAPTER EIGHT

Following the incredible breakfast earlier that morning, County had returned to bed for a much needed nap while Fernando spent some time with Moses. She met up with her husband at the pier where they'd soon set sail on the day's ice cruise.

The newlyweds approached each other slowly, yet County was smiling with love shining in her wide, expressive eyes. A bit of the brightness faded though when she noticed the drawn look that had taken hold of her husband's seductive caramel kissed features.

She frowned a little, smoothing her gloved hands up over the front of his white leather bomber jacket that made him appear more massive than he already was.

"Are you okay?" She asked.

Fernando took her hands and squeezed. "Did I say something wrong this morning?"

County's smile reflected a touch of cunning. "I don't recall you *saying* much."

His eye-crinkling smile emerged but briefly. "What I said about the threesome." He dipped his head to follow her face when she averted it suddenly.

"What'd I say?" He persisted.

"Is having a baby *that* important to you?" She asked.

He firmed his grip on her hands and gave her a jerk. "*You're* that important to me."

"But you want one?"

"Contessa…"

She ignored the warning in his heavy voice. "You do, don't you?"

Bowing his head, Fernando released County's hands and shoved his into the jacket's pockets.

"I did…" he said finally.

She blinked. "Did? What changed?"

"Why do you want to talk about this?" His mood had chilled and that had nothing to do with the fact that they were conversing in near sub-zero temps.

"How quickly we forget," she laughed drily, blinking off a wayward snow flake that had settled to her lashes. "*You* asked *me*, remember? And it wasn't even seven hours ago that you were talking about a baby. Now you're saying you *did* want one? What the fuck, Ramsey?"

He sighed, nodding his understanding of her frustration. "I know I'm confusing you but it's not about what you're thinking."

She grabbed the fuzzy collar of his jacket and jerked it. "So explain it to me!"

"Do I really have to, babe?" He spread his hands defensively. "I mean, you *have* met my father, right? You know what kind of monster he was and what kind of monsters he created."

County stepped back then, conjuring up images of Evangela Leer. She reached further back in her memory and summoned an image of the late Stefan Lyons.

"Kids can turn out so fucked up, even when they have the best parents. When they've got devil blood running through their veins…what's to expect?"

"Do you remember me saying almost the same thing about my father?" She challenged, hands going to her hips.

Fernando was massaging the bridge of his nose. "Your father isn't the devil," he sighed.

"But I was still concerned, thinking that his homosexuality might be inherited," she grimaced at her ignorance.

"Hmph...babe, if I was forced to choose, I'd rather have our kid turn out like your father than mine any day."

"Ramsey-"

"Stop." He'd moved close to lay a finger to her mouth. "Not now." He shook his head. "Too much of our time's been aggravated by foolishness. All I want is to enjoy my wife." He smiled at the way the fur-lined hood of her coat emphasized her pretty face.

"All I want is to give her pleasure and keep her close while we sail around on the ice."

"Heated pond," she corrected.

"Whatever." He kissed her sweetly-one peck to her mouth. "All I want is to thank God for the life I still have with you."

The lovers embraced and remained so until the rest of their party arrived.

***

Everyone agreed that the ice cruise was a unique and ethereal experience. The resort was truly an exquisite place made more exquisite by the mounds of fresh white powder that topped every building and dusted every limb.

Aboard a beautifully designed thirty foot yacht, some opted for taking in the view from the deck. Others enjoyed the beauty from the vessel's elegantly fashioned interior.

Nile; having grown up in a frigid climate, still opted for indoor observation. She'd gone to visit the cramped latrine and was leaving the equally cramped yet comfortable outer room when she literally ran into her husband.

"You okay?" Taurus' deep voice carried on a chuckle while his wife laughed brightly.

"I'm fine," she waved behind her. "Did you need to get in here?"

Rather grim faced all of a sudden, he shook his head. "Only came to look for you."

Impulsively, Nile grabbed his arm tugging at the sleeve of his sweatshirt to pull him back into the small area before she closed the door and set the lock.

"Nile what-"

"What is the matter with you?" She interrupted while pushing him down to the lilac marble counter. "I've been walking on eggshells hoping not to aggravate the mood you're in. Are you angry with me?"

"No," his striking gaze narrowed dangerously and he seemed appalled by the insinuation.

"Then what?" She gripped the tassels of his burgundy sweatshirt and jerked them a bit.

"Don't." He pleaded.

"What?" She insisted.

Muscles danced a sinful jig along his jaw and then he focused his bright eyes on a swirl in the paneling of the wall.

Taking pity when she saw the emotion sharpening his profile, she cupped his face and waited for him to look at her. "It's okay," she promised.

Taurus turned his face into her palm and kissed her there. "It's not. Not when I feel like hitting something when I see you fawning all over Quincee or wrapping gifts for Belle, Ty and Darby's babies and knowing that you can't ever..." he inhaled deeply and his words failed.

Further explanation wasn't necessary and Nile rested her forehead on his shoulder.

Taurus tugged a lock of her ebony hair. "I'm sorry for making you think I was upset with you."

"What can I do to make you understand that I'm alright with things as they are?"

"Hey," Taurus nudged her forehead from his shoulder and took her face in his hands. "You don't have to do a damn thing. You show me every day how much you've accepted how very unfair your life's been. Still makes me angry as hell," his voice sounded as grave as his expression appeared.

"It's up to me to get over this, love and I can't say it's gonna be easy. You're too good," he brushed the flawless onyx of her skin, "too much of an angel to have to accept something like that."

"But you do agree that angels deserve to be rewarded?" Her voice was almost a whisper.

"Definitely," he captured her mouth in a sweet, heartstopping kiss.

When it ended, Nile looked to the tassels on his shirt and batted them with her fingers. "So do you believe they deserve to get what they want?"

Taurus was about to respond in the resoundingly positive when he felt her at the drawstring of his black sweats.

"They um," his thoughts blurred when she cupped his crotch, "they deserve to get everything they want as often as they want it."

"Well then," she began a hungry suckle of his earlobe while removing him from the confines of his pants and boxers.

Taurus stood a bit to assist in the doffing of his clothes. Then, he aided in the removal of Nile's, reaching beneath her fuzzy pink and gray wool skirt to roll down the thick, cottony white tights she wore with pink and gray ski boots.

Nile held back nothing in her kiss, murmuring erotic words of pleasure and desire in her native tongue while helping Taurus tug away her underthings.

Feverishly, they arched closer, working to obtain prime positioning for what they wanted from one another. The boat suddenly dipped, knocking them apart and they began to laugh wildly.

When the gesture quieted, Taurus drew his wife across his lap. Nile pressed her lips together while raking her fingers through the extraordinary crop of his hair and then across sleek brows of the same light brown color. She moved on to brush her thumb across his incredible champagne tinged stare and then returned to chart the trail all over again.

Nile's breath hitched on a cry when Taurus guided himself into her. Again, she let her head rest to his shoulder. She cried into the fabric of the shirt responding to every plunge he gave her.

Her head fell back and she moaned her ecstasy into the air. Meanwhile, Taurus dragged his dazzling white teeth along the flawless molasses dark column of her neck, biting down softly. Nile's cries gained volume and became mixed in sobs of rich pleasure.

Taurus didn't try to silence her. His wife's inability to keep quiet was a potent arousal intensifier.

The door handle jiggled behind them followed by a knock.

"We're busy!" Taurus called.

"That wasn't nice," Nile moaned and then bit her lip as the waves of orgasm began to build inside her.

"You're the angel, not me," his voice was muffled in her neck yet his wicked smile was just visible where his sensually crafted mouth curved. Love flooded his bright eyes yet again when Nile's laughter filled his ears.

***

The excursion into town during the ice cruise was like a trip into the past. The village was a quaint place that reminded everyone of the lovely Scottish borough that Kraven and Darby had called home.

The group enjoyed a terrific lunch. There was light shopping for everyone except Sabra. Smoak had to hoist her over his shoulder and carry her from a boutique that sold nothing but boots.

The crowd set sail at dusk and just in time to capture the sight of the colorful lights that were beginning to shimmer in honor of the season. On the yacht, the couples scattered to find their own little niches from which to enjoy the view and quite moments alone.

~~~

"Did you have something to do with this?" Johari asked when Moses escorted her to a spot at the boat's stern. The area was already set up with a few thick coverlets and a bucket chilling a bottle of wine and a few bottles of Moses' favorite beer.

"Not at all," he pretended that he was just as surprised to find the romantic arrangement. "Don't guess we should let it go to waste though, huh? Hope the wine's alright for you." He went to investigate the offerings.

"Oh no wine for me," Johari tugged on the fringed edge of the brick red scarf she wore and got herself comfortable on the thickly cushioned seating.

Beneath a hooded pitch stare, Moses watched her drawing the cover across jean clad legs. "It'll help keep you warm," he encouraged.

"That's okay."

"Come on Twig, you can't have me over here drinking by myself."

"Ram?" She gave a quick toss of her sandy red hair and frowned playfully. "Are you trying to get me drunk?"

"Off one glass of wine?" He shook his head once decisively. "I don't think one glass'll do that."

"I thought the same thing once," as if realizing she'd spoken aloud, she cleared her throat and posted a bright smile. "Have your drink, Ram. In fact-" she pushed off the coverings and scooted to the edge of the seat. Reaching for Moses, she pulled him down next to her and prepared his beer bottle herself.

"There," she pressed the chilled, uncapped Killian's Red into his hand and then snuggled against him and sighed her contentment.

Moses felt anything but content. His unsettling strikingly attractive features were then drawn into a tense almost menacing mask. Absently, he smoothed his mouth across the tendrils of the fine hair at his wife's temple.

***

"Not bad, huh?" Quest asked when he joined Michaela at a quiet end along one side of the yacht's wood grained railing.

"Yeah..." she rubbed her hands along her sweater sleeves enjoying the warming effect as they brushed the fuzzy black fabric. "Ty really hooked us up."

She kept watch over the stunning view for a few more seconds and then bowed her head. "Quest...I love Ty. I'm truly happy for her and Quay."

"But?" Quest turned his back on the view and leaned on the rail. Bowing his head as well, he focused on his navy blue hiking boots one folded over the other.

"I love you," he said when his probe generated no response.

Mick raised her head staring at him as if he'd shocked her. "I know that," she whispered fiercely.

"Then you know that nothing you say to me will change that, right?"

"I don't want another baby."

He nodded once, keeping his eyes steady with hers to show that he'd already reached that conclusion.

"I love Quincee," again Mick's voice carried on the same fierceness. "I'd die for her- happily." She looked back toward the gentle water and the white waves of snow beyond it.

"Every time I look at her I see how much she loves me. Quest I really don't know what I'd do if that look ever went away."

He was pulling her to him then, drawing her closer to stand between his thighs.

"That look *won't* ever go away," he vowed.

"I think I got lucky with Quinn," She nodded as though trying to resolve the fact in her mind. "I don't want to risk a second child and-" She squeezed her eyes shut. When she opened them, the amber orbs sparkled with unshed tears. "I don't think I have enough love in me for two- or more..." she swallowed.

"Are you serious?" The question carried on short laughter. "You've got more reason than anyone to shut down your emotions." He bent lower to look more directly into her eyes. "In spite of all that, you've got more love inside you than any woman- any*one* I know."

"My mother-"

"You are not your mother." He jerked her none-too-gently then. "You are not your mother."

"That may be," she brushed her thumb across the sultry curve of his mouth and smiled wanly. "But I know I'm not strong enough. I can feel it."

"Is that why you've been pushing me away this entire trip?"

"I forgot my pills," she toyed with the silver zipper tab of the denim jacket he wore over his hoody. "Something told me I wouldn't be able to get you to wear a condom."

"Something told you correctly," he confirmed in a stony tone. "When you say that you're not strong enough, is that why you don't want another child or do you just not want another baby for any reason?"

Her laughter was mingled with a sob. "I like it just being the three of us right now but..." she pressed her lips together as if summoning strength. "Even if I wanted more, I honestly don't think I could handle it-too afraid I'd turn out like...her. She only had enough inside her to love Nile."

As much as she hated to cry, that's exactly what she did then. It was as if the admission shed the last of the unconscious wall she'd built around the issue.

"Hey," Quest stood and embraced her tight, rocking her slow as she cried into his chest. "What the hell do you think I'm here for?" He asked when she began to quiet. "We're here to make each other strong, you know?"

He bent again, cupping her face in his hands while she sniffled and blinked tear remnants from her lashes.

"If you're never ready, then you're never ready. I love you- you and Quincee are more than I ever thought I'd have to call my own. But if the reason you're standing here in front of me so terrified is because you think you're not strong enough then, I'm here to tell you that this isn't a one person job if you ever decide you'd like to add to our threesome. I meant it when I said you were never getting rid of me."

Again, she began to cry. "Dammit…"

"Shut up," he whispered and pulled her into a kiss that mingled with her tears.

***

Johari jerked herself awake, realizing she'd fallen asleep in Moses' arms while they enjoyed the view from their end of the yacht.

"I get why you're afraid to drink-falling asleep at the drop of a hat this way."

Her smile soured. "I'm not afraid." She could withstand less of a minute beneath the knowing glare Moses had perfected.

"Damn you, Ram," she wrenched out of his loose embrace and left the deck in a huff.

Blindly, she stormed through the yacht until she slammed her way past the first closed door she found. Laughter rolled into a despairing wave when she discovered where she was.

"Nice goin' Jo," she studied the large bed in the master cabin. Her ears twitched at the sound of the door opening and closing softly behind her.

"This was thoughtful of you, Twig."

"Hmph," Johari turned to her husband. "Just like a Ramsey. You insult me and now believe I'm about to have sex with you."

Moses smoothed both hands across his shaved dark head while he strolled further into the cabin. "First off, yes I do believe you're about to have sex with me. Second, I didn't insult you. I only pointed out a fact. You're upset because I stumbled onto it."

"Stumbled onto what?" She slapped her hands to her thighs. "You're wrong." She threw back when he only looked at her.

"Since you think so, correct me." He challenged.

Weary then, Johari let her eyelids flutter close. She moved deeper into the spacious teakwood paneled cabin until she'd come up against the roll top desk in the corner. "I should be over this by now."

Moses came to haunch over, caging her with his body when he set a hand on either side of her against the desk top.

"Tell me," he nuzzled his face into her neck.

"You already know I'm not afraid to drink- it's what drinking reminds me of." She turned amidst the bounds of his arms. "You know how I lost our baby…how much drinking had to do with it." She sat on the desk. "Being around all this baby stuff the past few days…"

"Christ…" Moses rolled his eyes and then sat next to her on the big desk. "Twig, I'm sorry."

"Don't be please. Please," she curved her hand around his elbow and tugged. "I guess I haven't buried all this as deeply as I've tried."

"Chances are, *that's* the trouble." He took her hand from the sleeve of the gray corduroy top shirt he wore and squeezed. "This isn't something you bury."

"Oh? Right!" She laughed. "And obviously bringing it all to the surface is working so well for me."

"That's because you're trying to run from it." He ignored her sarcasm. "You forget I know what good and what damage running does."

"I was so stupid, Ram." She hugged herself to ward off sudden chill. "I didn't realize what a miracle I had and now…"

"Stop it, Twig." Moses rose to his feet and bent over her again. "We were kids- scared and making mistakes left and right. I'd say *now* we're old enough to know better, don't you?"

Smiling a smile as sweet as the emotion in her eyes, Johari brushed her fingers along one side of Moses' breathtaking dark face. Nodding, she leaned close to slide a kiss from his cheek to his ear.

Moses palmed her neck and drew her into what he deemed a more suitable kiss. Johari was so involved in the act that she'd yet to tune into the goings on below her waist. That is, until she felt his fingers inside her.

"Ram, we can't-"

"Why the hell not?" He followed every change in her expression and smiled when she moaned. "If it makes you feel better, we won't use the bed."

Before Johari could request clarification, he'd hoisted her high and set her to a wall near the cabin window. Kneeling reverently, he dragged her denims and tights down toned café-au-lait thighs.

Molding his perfectly shaped head to her hands, Johari twisted her hips when he nuzzled her core with his nose.

It wasn't enough. Johari felt the stirrings of climax and softly begged him not to move before she peaked. He ignored her plea however, taking great delight in driving her crazy with the arousal she carried for him.

Her jeans and underthings were down around one black leather ankle boot. The other was free of her clothing and that allowed Johari to link her leg about Moses' lean waist.

Clothing fell in a fast tangle. Moses' garments rested around the gray suede Timberlands he sported. Johari quickly discarded her scarf, jacket and sweater. Moses did the same with his clothing and she reveled in the seductively intimidating artwork that adorned his body. His tattoos rippled and swayed against the muscles packing the deep ebony of his skin.

He'd nestled his face between her lace covered breasts. Obsessed with her scent, he inhaled cupping a breast in one hand, a thigh in the other.

Shamelessly, Johari begged him still. He didn't ignore her that time, taking her in a long filling stroke that stopped her breath. He abandoned the breast he'd captured and was then cradling both her buttocks in his wide palms steadying her to his satisfaction as he thrust up into her.

The pressure of the thrusts sent Johari's head bumping back into the wall and she welcomed it. Reddish tresses fell loose of the French braid and tumbled about her face while she moaned over the savory lunges of his sex. She gripped the orgasm inducing erection inside her drenched walls and applied a strong massage to his every stroke.

Moses planted a fist against the wall while cradling her ass in one hand-an effortless show of grace. The depth of his intimate surges and the flood of her moisture soaking his shaft drew him feverishly close to a release he desperately craved but wasn't ready for. He needed to be hard, deep and soaked inside her for much, much longer.

CHAPTER NINE

The dazzling ice cruise was sure to be on everyone's minds for quite some time. The group all agreed that the resort owners definitely had what was sure to be a sought after treat for future guests. The event was so deliciously exhausting in fact that everyone decided that the next couple of days would be devoted to a deeper level of rest and relaxation.

Everyone took the decision to heart and only ventured outside their suites for a bit of breakfast or lunch. Suppers were delivered to each suite. The couples enjoyed their meals before the stone fireplaces that gave off warmth as well as cozy golden glows of illumination.

~~~~

Yohan had gotten up to look for his wife and found her on their balcony. He enjoyed the sight of her wrapped in a heavy navy blue flannel robe.

"Need company?" He called when she sensed his presence.

Melina turned away from the snow covered mountain range in the distance. "Was just on my way back inside," she wrapped the robe more snuggly about her small frame.

The downtrodden tone to her response didn't go unnoticed by Yohan. "It's alright if you want time to yourself, Meli."

"No. Han, it's fine," she bit her lip as if suddenly unsure.

Yohan pushed a big shoulder off the door frame and strolled across the balcony to claim one of the large deep armchairs. Melina watched as he made himself comfortable. She marveled over the awesome cut of his build, her slanting stare wandering across the unyielding blackberry wall that was his chest. She wondered if the frigid cold even penetrated the range of abs, pects and biceps.

Yohan relaxed on the chair as though he were enjoying a warm day on the beach. He patted a hand to his thigh. The wide granite length was covered by a pair of navy sleep pants that matched his robe in which Melina was presently garbed.

Dutifully, she accepted the silent offer. She straddled his lap instead of just taking up position on one thigh.

"Great trip, huh?" He asked simply to begin conversation until she decided to confide in him. He didn't have long to wait.

"I want a baby," she blurted.

The look claiming Yohan's magnificently blended features proved that he was beyond stunned.

Melina bowed her head, but had no intentions of giving into cowardice. She'd already exposed herself. May as well complete the job, she figured.

"I know you don't want one and I can accept that," she cupped her palms about his face. "And I've never been so happy. I once thought we'd never have another chance to be so happy. I'm not trying to upset that, but you can tell I'm acting weird and you deserve to know why."

Yohan shifted a bit in the chair and rested a few fingers alongside his temple once she'd pulled back from him. "Why do you think I don't want a baby, Meli?"

She appeared stumped for a moment. "Don't you remember what you said after Quay went off on you guys about Ty?"

"And you took that to mean I'd be...what? Upset if you were pregnant?" He smothered her elbows in his hands when he held her there. "Is there something you want to tell me, Mel?"

"No," she shook her head, "there's not. I swear. I-I just...I wouldn't do that without talking to you about it first, Han. I just need to know how you'd feel about it...if it happened...would you...want it?" She bit her lip to stop her rambling.

He bowed his head to rub his fingers through the pitch waves of the low cut afro he sported. "When you left me, I cursed myself everyday- more than once a day for not getting you pregnant." He shrugged, beautiful dark features tensing into an unreadable mask. "It was stupid, but I thought it'd make you stay.

"No Mel, I wouldn't be upset if you had my baby in there," bottomless midnight eyes focused on the robe where it parted to reveal her chocolate skin and hint of bosom. He took her elbows again. "Are we good?"

Melina nodded, sending the coarse waves of her hair bouncing merrily into her face and slanting gaze. "We're good." She felt as though the weight of her concerns had vanished. "Are you ready to go back inside?" She shivered a tad.

Yohan inclined his head and fixed her with confusion in his stare. "Don't you want a baby?"

Her lips parted.

"There's only one way we're gonna get one, you know?"

Dumbfounded, Melina sat there straddling his lap and still trying to figure him out. Suddenly her lashes settled like hummingbird wings and she shuddered on a moan. His hand was inside the robe, his thumb working her clit into a nub of sensation.

"Han," his name was a faint murmur on her mouth. She could feel the incredible ridge of his sex tense and lengthen against her. Slowly, she worked her body on his, crying out when the tip of his thumb disappeared inside her.

Yohan relaxed with his head back on the chair, taking his pleasure in the emotion commanding her beautiful dark face. As more of her erotic juices coated his thumb, the more his restraint weakened.

He didn't have long to ponder his ability to go slow. Melina freed him from the snap front of his sleep pants and took him inside her in one slow, seamless move.

Yohan closed his eyes. For a third time, he took her elbows to control her moves, bending her to his approval. Mel had no complaints, happy to let him guide her along his erection. Eventually, mind and body were on the same pleasure-numbed plane.

***

Warm milk had; without a doubt, become one of Tykira's favorite indulgences since the onset of pregnancy. In her opinion, it was a pretty boring thing to crave. Most of the women she knew had such elaborate cravings as pickles with ice cream or pickled pig's feet and peanut butter.

Laughter bubbled up inside her while she stirred the pot of slowly heating milk. She enjoyed the wintry view and savored the peacefulness from the kitchen island where she worked.

"Dammit Ty…"

"So much for that." She sighed, having heard her husband's growled complaint.

"What's it gonna take to keep you on your ass and off your feet?" Quay strolled barefoot into the kitchen.

"No. Here," Ty turned the tables when he came over to move her from the stove and assume command of the milk prep. She pushed him down to a stool nearest the stove.

"Quay...baby this has got to stop. You're getting on mine and everybody else's damned nerves." She leaned over to press a kiss to his mouth when he blinked as if hurt. "Honey I love you for caring, but you can't keep going overboard like this. You do and *I'm* gonna kill you before you have the chance to meet your little girls."

She caught his burgundy T-shirt in a fist and tugged threateningly. "I swear I'll do it Quay- quick and easy in your sleep." Her smile reflected pure cunning while her captivating almond shaped eyes narrowed. "That last bit should reassure you that I won't over exert myself while getting the job done."

"Jesus Tyke," Quay tilted his head to massage the bridge of his nose. "I'm sorry," he smiled in spite of himself.

Ty took pity. "I'm alright," she laughed softly and nudged her nose with his. "I feel great and Dr. Jentry isn't concerned about anything either."

"I know that Tyke. I know that," he reached out to rub her swollen stomach beneath a bubble gum pink PJ top. "When Q told me what happened in Scotland-the fear he felt...I felt it too," he brought his smoldering gaze to her face then. "All I could think about was how easily it all could've gone down so much differently- so much worse."

"Quay..." she grazed her fingertips through his close cropped waves. "Honey we weren't even there."

"It was still too close to home," he took her hand and squeezed. "You know that."

"Shh..." she nodded, pressing her head to his in hopes of easing his mind and heart. Then she smirked. "Know what?" She took the pot from the burner. "I suddenly don't want milk anymore."

"Nah Tyke, don't," he rubbed his hands up and down the sleeves of her powder blue chenille robe. "I shouldn't have interrupted you."

"Well it's too late 'cause I don't want it." She linked her arms about his neck. "I'm in the mood for something stronger and chocolate."

Quay blinked, the rich onyx of his stare reflected sudden understanding. "Tyke…"

She was already pulling him to his feet.

"Tykira…"

"Quaysar…"

~~~~

"How about a back rub?" Quay was attempting to strike a bargain as they entered the suite.

Ty's throaty laughter filled the room. "You're gonna have to do better than that."

"I don't want to hurt you." His low voice carried on an uncertain chord.

"Do you recall what I said about hurting *you*?" She sat down on their unmade bed and pulled him down next to her.

"Ty…" her name was a whisper on his perfectly defined lips. She pulled him into a delicate kiss before he could say more.

With mock uncertainty, her tongue coaxed his to come out and play. Gently, hers darted out to outline his mouth and then just past to stroke the velvety softness there and onward to test the texture of his tongue.

Again, Quay spoke her name as though he were desperate to hold on to his intention to refuse her. Lost in her own wants; and having little interest in her husband's concerns, Ty pulled him down to lie next to her. Her kiss gained in lust and need.

Quay was past the point of wanting his wife beyond reason. He drove his tongue down her throat hungrily with mounting intensity once she moaned her approval.

Instinctively, Ty reached for his hand bringing it to the square bodice of her PJ top. She arched, biting her lip on the sensation his fingers ignited when they curved about an achy, itchy nipple. She wrenched her mouth from his and began a sultry nibble of his earlobe.

"Quay, do more…do more please…"

The breathy request clipped away the final tether on his resistance. He groaned something obscene into her mouth and gave himself over to the arousal stirred by her plump breast overflowing his palm.

Greedy and impatient, Ty took his hand and dragged it to the spot that most wanted his focus. She cried out shamelessly when he gave her what she asked for. Soon though, she wanted more than his fingers stroking her puckered sex into sensual oblivion and she reached for him inside his PJ bottoms.

Quay's long sleek brows were drawn close as he worked over a nipple suckling and moaning his approval over the way the bud firmed beneath his tongue. His mouth slackened on the nub at the feel of her hand inside his pants.

"Ty…fuck…"

"Yes please…"

"No…" he tried to shake his head, but most of his strength had deserted him. "No Ty, mmm…" he grew more rigid while she worked his shaft in her hand.

"Ty, no."

"You don't mean that," she whispered the medley of words, sweeping her thumb across the wide satiny head of his undeniable erection. Pre-release pooled at the tip.

"Ty please-"

"Just give me what I want and I'll stop." With that said, she pushed him back in order to resituate herself on her side. In the spooning embrace she rubbed her bottom against the breathtaking throb of his bare erection.

"Dammit..." he groaned the word into her milk chocolate toned shoulder while he relieved her of her underthings. "Dammit...dammit, Ty..." he sank deep inside her from behind. "Please tell me I'm not hurting you..."

"Far from it," her breath hitched on a gasp as he extended the penetration. "Far from it," she promised.

"Thank God..." he cupped her breast, perfect teeth grazed or gnawed her shoulder as he pumped into her.

Ty reciprocated by grinding into his ravenous thrusts with her own brand of eagerness. She then angled her head back to kiss him raggedly.

Their lovemaking lasted well into the morning.
***

Pike woke that morning to find that his wife had already headed out for breakfast. Downstairs, they had time to only speak a few words to one another. Still, what little time they had together was enough to tell Pike that the tension he'd sensed from his wife wasn't all part of his imagination.

Sabella was distant which was very evident when he pulled her into a morning kiss that easily melded into something more involved. Subtly, yet noticeably she eased out of the kiss.

"Can I fix you a plate?" She patted his whisker roughened cheek.

"Thanks," the reply was casual enough but Pike spent the bulk of his time watching her instead of eating.

Belle had finished off a pitifully lacking plate of dry toast and a few strips of bacon. Then, she rushed off with Nile and Contessa for a walk around the grounds that was to be followed by a quick trip into town.

It was well past lunch when it looked like he'd finally have a moment alone with her.

Belle was in their suite, agitation shimmering on her beautiful pecan brown face as she sifted through one lovely article of clothing after another.

"Forgot something?" Pike inquired, while walking into the room, hands clasped behind his back.

"Trying to find something to wear for this engagement party," she grimaced and all but threw a gorgeous deep purple off shoulder gown to the bed. "Nothing's 'doing it' for me."

Pike passed an armchair and paused to rub his finger across the gauzy material of a stunning chiffon over satin evening gown. "Guess I won't be any help there," he said, "I rather see you in absolutely nothing." He glanced up in time to see her rolling her eyes.

The reaction was enough to drain whatever patience he had left. Grinding down on his jaw muscle so viciously that it jumped, he bolted over and snatched away the dress she'd just picked up.

"Isak-" Additional words died on her tongue as it was suddenly occupied by his kiss.
"Wait-"

"I have."

The roughly voiced words shuddered through Belle and then she was falling into the well of pleasure he never failed to create when he touched her.

"Kiss me back."

The order made her whimper yet she complied most willingly. Her fingers tunneled into the forest of ebony silk that was his hair, the texture massaging her skin as luxuriously as his tongue massaged hers. She was so thoroughly beneath his spell, that it was some time before she realized he'd unbuttoned her frost blue blouse.

Belle felt his hands on her bare flesh and discovered he'd undone the front clasp on her bra as well.

"Stop," she gasped the word in tandem with slamming her hands against his solid chest.

Pike barely registered the blow and merely stepped before her when she tried to move past him.

"Isak-"

"Why did you stop me?"

She waved a hand behind her. "The party-"

"Bullshit."

"Then what do you want to hear?" She snapped in a fierce whisper, her expressive eyes narrowing in accusation. "What Isak? That I've spent years working on my figure and when I'm finally on the verge of getting one, I'm losing it again?"

He seemed frozen for the span of a few seconds and then dragged a hand through his hair and tugged. "What the hell are you talking about?"

Belle pressed her fingers to the corners of her eyes, silently bemoaning the way she'd let her emotions get the best of her.

"I'm just being stupid."

"Agreed," He lifted a long brow in challenge when she looked at him. "I still want to know what this is."

"Isak-" She made to move past him again but he planted a hand on the wall next to her and prevented any escape. Accepting her imprisonment, she went about buttoning her shirt. A low rumble from his throat warned her against any such action. Swallowing her disagreement, she folded her arms across the open shirt and did her best to shield herself from his glare.

"Do you remember the night I saw you at dinner with Martin and Arthur?" She referenced her theatre colleagues Martin Victors and Arthur Prince.

Pike gave a brief nod, intrigue settling in place of frustration.

Belle drew back a few thick ringlets of her hair and grimaced. "As terrified as I was about why you were there…when you noticed how much weight I'd lost." She shrugged dejectedly. "I was thrilled."

The low rumble resumed in Pike's throat and Belle risked a quick look in his direction.

"I know you didn't approve," her gaze faltered at what she saw in his bottomless eyes. "I'm sorry Isak, but I don't want to lose that feeling. I don't want you seeing me…like this… anymore." She voiced the last word in a whisper and then risked another look at him. She wondered at the soft expression he wore.

"I don't believe this bullshit."

She blinked, expecting anything other than the stoic hardness of his words.

"Isak-"

"Shut up," he stood closer an effectively intimidating stance given his size. "You're carrying my child."

"I know that Isak, I-"

"Be quiet," his voice was softer yet no less threatening. "Clearly, you have no idea how stupidly happy that makes me and how much more it makes me want to be inside you."

"Isak-"

"I can't believe you think I'm shallow enough to turn away from you because…" he couldn't finish the statement and averted his gaze toward the floor.

Belle swallowed. She was mesmerized by; and more than a little unsettled by the muscle jumping fiercely along his jawline. When he spoke, his voice was so low that she almost had to strain to hear it.

"You know how I feel about you, Bella. You know there's nothing you can say to me that will change that, but baby I'm done with this. I'm done trying to prove to you that you're it for me." He dropped his hand and withdrew from her personal space.

"I guess I'll let you figure out that part on your own this time."

Immobile, Belle watched him turn and head out of the room. "Isak!" She called and got the door slamming at his back in response.

CHAPTER TEN

That night, the grounds crew put on a dazzling fireworks display for their exclusive guests. The show was actually doubling as a dress rehearsal of sorts for the crew when the resort officially opened. Nevertheless, the current guests had no complaints and found the show among the most impressive they'd seen.

From the rooftop terrace, the couples enjoyed the awesome sights that lit up the night sky. Cuddled in deep, oversized chairs they sat close to the large, brick encased fire pit at the center of the terrace. The event was made even more enjoyable by the array of drinks and scrumptious appetizers that had been provided.

~~~

"Hey…" Sabra whined when Smoak thwarted her intention to take another sip of the rum laced cocoa she'd grown a tad bit addicted to.

He placed the mug on the wrought iron endtable nearest their chair. Then he enfolded Sabra more securely against him. The move quelled any complaints she was gearing up to make.

"I don't give one damn about whatever shit is goin' on in your family or mine or in that business of yours." His voice was low and shiver-inducing against her ear. "You're mine after your aunt's wedding."

Sabra giggled, content from head to toe. She turned her face into Smoak's wool coffee brown jacket sleeve and inhaled the familiar, beckoning scent of his cologne. "Be sure you tell that to your partner in crime. I swear that Lee Lee doesn't know how to give me a break."

Smoak's sly grin was a breathtaking stark white contrast against the flawless ebony of his skin. "Are you telling me that this control freak attitude of yours is all Lee Lee's fault?"

"Absolutely," she spoke the lie without shame. "Besides," she added once his resulting laughter had somewhat settled. "I'm already all yours."

"Not in every way," some of the humor had gone from his clear voice. "I never should've let us go on like that for so long but I plan to correct it- and soon."

Sabra angled her head up and back to fix her smoky brown gaze on his face. "You really want to be stuck with me forever?"

"In every way," he kissed her nose. "I love you."

"I love you." She murmured the confession into his jaw.

***

Across the way in their own little haven of intimacy, Kraven and Darby enjoyed the fireworks and their time together as well. They swayed to the seductive jazz arrangements that piped up onto the terrace and relished the contentment of their embrace.

Just then however, Darby was in the process of gaping at the garnet encrusted thumb ring Kraven had presented as he wished her a Happy Christmas.

"I hope you don't think this is gonna double as my birthday present." She smiled while studying her birthstone adorning the platinum band. "I expect something just as fabulous as this ring then too."

"I swear it's not a double gift." He spoke the words into her temple.

"So if it's not a double gift…is it a bribe to make me forget that you didn't tell me why you were brooding the other day?"

"Lass…"

"Come on," she tugged the lapels of the mahogany suede jacket he wore over a cream shirt. "I confessed my troubles, now it's *your* turn."

Kraven nodded, sending heavy tufts of lush brown hair onto his forehead while he conceded her point. "If Hill calls, I'll have to go."

Darby's mouth thinned but she nodded. She'd already prepared herself to hear those words, but that didn't make *actually* hearing them any easier.

"I know why you feel you have to," she fisted her hands against his chest in a show of acceptance instead of anger. "Doesn't mean I have to like it."

Kraven's sinfully alluring features tightened at her admission. "Do you think I like it any better, Lass? I want to stay home and watch you fill with my child. I want to run out like a damn fool to the market trying to find all the disgusting things you'll have cravings for." He laughed shortly in spite of himself and then grew solemn.

"If Hill calls, if there's…some way for us to put down what threatens our families-" He closed his eyes and brought his forehead to hers.

"I know what people say about blood lust, especially what they say about mine- so be it." He toyed with a tassel from her gray and black plaid hoody and then brushed his mouth across hers.

"You've had your blood, the dogs got theirs, I want mine…as much as that bothers me…I still want it."

Darby could see him struggling as if there were more he wanted to say. She waited for him to continue.

"Does that upset you?" he finally asked her.

She stood on her toes then, cupping his face and smiling when a sudden wind blew a few curls into her face. "I can't see myself being upset because you want your family and friends safe. But I won't lie to you- I'm very selfish. I want you with me and the only way I'll get through you *not* being with me…the only way I'll get through whatever's to come is if you don't shut me out."

His nod was a singular up and down move. "I get it."

"Get something else," she tugged his lapel again. "Until Hill makes his call, you're all mine. I expect you to make up *in advance* for whatever time hunting down those bitches takes from me."

"Well then," the dangerously sexy grin emerged on his striking face then. "You know I'm always happy to be used in whatever way you see fit."

***

After the fireworks, everyone ventured back inside the house to get warm. The girls scattered here and there while the guys collected in the den down the hall from the main room. There, the talk was politics, sports or other forms of entertainment. Drinks and laughter flowed as easily as the conversation.

Pike nursed a vodka rocks while listening in as Yohan and Quaysar squared off in a debate of the year's football season. When Moses nudged his shoulder and pointed toward the door, he saw Belle at the front of the room.

Wringing her hands, she appeared uncertain and as though she wanted to be anywhere else. He watched her, quietly appraising the emerald green sarong style dress that fell past her ankles and dragged the floor. How could she think she was anything less than spectacular? He wondered and worked to keep his face an unreadable mask. Standing then, he made his way to her on slow deliberate steps.

Sabella appeared even more uneasy when he stood right before her. "Can we talk?"

"About what?"

The firm chord of his voice rattled something inside her, but she wouldn't allow it the power to sway her determination. "Please Isak?"

He studied her beneath a narrowed gaze and then downed the rest of his drink. With a wave of the empty glass, he directed her toward the den door. Silently, he followed along as she led the way down the quiet corridor to a closed door at the end.

The reading room, unoccupied for the moment, was fragranced with a mix of potpourri from silver dishes dotting the room. The logs from the blazing fire filled the space with warmth, aroma and a golden glow.

Pike shut the door behind them and set his glass to a glass table. The unexpected clatter made Belle jump and she knew he wouldn't make this easy for her. Turning resignedly, she decided to just get it all out and be done with it.

"Isak, I'm sorry. I'm so sorry," she clutched her hands while professing the apology. "I've been wrong on so many levels, but mostly for letting you believe that I was upset because I think your feelings for me might change. I believe you want me-as I am-forever and I believe that'll never change."

"But?"

"*But*," she sighed, reciprocating his prompt. "Being insecure isn't an easy thing to let go of after a lifetime of it," she went to warm her hands at the fire.

"When we were married…before…I never really let go of it then either. It wasn't a strong feeling but it was still there and I've been trying-" her breath hitched, the confession overwhelming her.

"I've been trying Isak, but it's so hard," she gave a quick bewildered shake of her head, "things hit me out of nowhere and throw me right back into that uncertain, self-conscious imbecile I used to be- hmph…still am…I guess…"

"Bella…" he spanned the distance separating them and pulled her close. He was glad she'd turned her back for it allowed him to shed the stoic look he'd tried to maintain.

His heart broke for her. The lost tone in her voice had taken him back to that terrifying day in Italy when he almost lost her forever.

"This might be hard for you to believe but I really am happier than I've ever been," she sniffled softly. "I'm so excited about the future and I can't wait until it's time for the baby." She shook her head again. "Every night I pray nothing happens to jeopardize it and here I am harping on old anxieties instead of thanking God for what I have."

"Shh…" he nuzzled his face into her chestnut brown curls and rocked her for a while.

"Those old anxieties are a part of you, you know?"

She sniffled again. "I don't want them to be."

Pike turned her to him, cupping her face as he peered into her eyes. "They will be as long as you try to fight them by yourself. I want to help, but I need you to come to me. I promise that I want to share it all- all the beautiful," he brushed his thumb across the corner of her eye.

"The phenomenal," he continued, resting his hand over the bump their child was making inside her, "and the upsetting," he set his forehead to hers.

"Won't you let me in? Let me carry you, while you deal with it. I swear you won't scare me."

Sabella laughed some through her tears and she nodded.

"Isak?" She called once they'd swayed in their embrace for a time. "Can we sit here for a while?"

Slowly, Pike lifted his head to observe their beautiful romantic surroundings. A bit of doubt shadowed his unfairly magnificent features. "All you want to do in here is sit?" he asked.

Belle stepped out of their embrace then. She backed away until she was in the middle of the elaborately designed Persian rug before the fireplace. She'd pulled him along with her and gave him a soft shove down to a deep sandstone armchair at the edge of the rug.

"To start," she told him. Keeping hold of his hand for support, she slowly lowered to her knees before him.

Pike leaned close, wanting to kiss her but Belle resisted, urging him instead to recline in the chair. She inched closer and with agonizing slowness, unfastened his trousers. She'd tugged the zipper only halfway down before moving up to ply him with a lengthy kiss. She offered just a faint stroke of her tongue before settling back to her task below his waist.

Pike wanted to ensure her comfort, yet words deserted him when she took him in her mouth. She moaned ever so slightly as she suckled him slow.

Her lips pleasured only the wide head of his deep bronzed shaft. A feeling of immense power and pleasure welled inside her when she whimpered and seemed to melt into the chair's cushions. His groan was intense yet carried a breathy quality that further stoked Belle's pleasure. She filled her mouth with him, swallowing around the choking sensation when his size threatened to stifle her breath.

Isak dropped a hand to the glossy ringlets of her hair, easing the mass to one side. He wanted to see her captivating face as she treated him. Reflexively, his hand fisted in her hair and he began the slightest thrusts against her tongue. He groaned louder each time she dragged it along his shaft.

"Belle-" his head fell back to the chair while his hips pumped at a faster pace. Her soft moans as she suckled and bathed his erection, had turned every part of him- save one- to a limp mass of sensation. Again, his hand tightened in her hair and he knew he was on the verge of losing whatever control he had left.

Sabella murmured a few disapproving words when Pike set her away. She didn't dare argue further once she spied the determination in his smoldering pitch stare. Gently, he put her on her back and set his knee between her thighs to keep them parted.

He jerked out of the royal blue shirt he wore over a black tee and then brushed his fingers across her dress.

"You can get out of this or I can take you out of it. If I do it, you may not be able to wear it again."

"There's a zipper on the side," she offered the helpful bit of information. Judging the look he gave her, she decided the effort might prove to be too much for him.

She tugged at the gold zipper, gradually revealing more of her beautiful pecan brown skin to his view. Pike studied his wife as though he were seeing her for the first time. He finished the unzipping when she eased the tab down as far as she could, given that his body practically stifled any other movement save the subtle grinds she made against the knee snug at her center.

Pike took her out of the dress. All the while, he studied her face seeking any signs of uncertainty or self-consciousness. There were none. He smiled approvingly while bringing his dark head down over her.

Pike's seductively shaped mouth grazed Belle's full breasts. He refused to take in her nipples regardless of how insistently she nudged them to his lips. Instead, his mouth charted a steady path downward until he was there at the treasure that was his alone to enjoy.

Belle arched her back when his tongue filled her; stroked her with every inch he drove home. He spaced her thighs to his satisfaction and then rested flat on the rug where she lay. Hungrily, he feasted on her femininity. The taste and smell of her only increased his hunger. Belle felt her breathing grow labored as his head moved with a ravenous intensity between her legs. He took her with maddening, lengthy probes that had her flexing the walls of her sex as she worked to draw out every ounce of pleasure he gave.

She pleaded with him to give her more. Her hand splayed out across the rug and then over the rich burnished gold coloring of his heaving chest and back. She knew he was carrying her to the brink of ultimate pleasure, but that he would torture her at length before rewarding her with that prize.

Restless, needy and passion filled, Belle dragged her fingers through her hair and bucked insistently against him. She was happy to take whatever pleasure he'd let her have before he denied her and made her beg again.

The pop and snap of the fire was the perfect accompaniment to the gasps and low moans from the two lovers doused in molten illumination.

Pike rose up to kiss her and Belle curved her hand around his sex. She worked it up and down his rigid length in hopes of turning him as insane with need as she was.

There was no need. Pike was already far gone. The kiss had turned fierier and he continued to lunge his tongue deeper until she whimpered around it in response to his sex invading hers. Belle cupped her hands at his waist and then down to his ass. The perfectly toned buttocks sat above the waistband of the jeans he hadn't bothered to fully remove as claimed her vigorously.

"Couldn't wait for me, huh?" he quietly, playfully chastised having felt her coming all over his erection.

"Complaints?" Her response was an airy whisper.

Pike chuckled low for only a moment. "Not one," he said before he came hard and lost all ability to speak.

***

Contessa rested her fingers against the edge of the slim rectangular box as though she feared being bitten if she moved them any further.

She gave an obvious swallow, her coffee brown stare still on the box. "I thought we were gonna wait 'til Christmas?"

Fernando shrugged lazily beneath the loose, rust colored knit sweater he wore. His bright eyes scanned the ruby encrusted gold choker before he looked over at his wife. "I guess it's the whole next day not being promised and time waiting for no man thing that made me want to do it now."

"Mmm," she nodded, "and being shot probably had a lot to do with it as well."

"Right..." he laughed, "almost forgot about that."

"Your present is upstairs."

He grinned. "In bed?" his tone was hopeful.

"In a box."

The sly grin combined with a leer. "I've seen that box and I like it very much."

"You're disgusting."

"You like it."

Contessa slapped her hand against the back of the sofa. "Come on Ramsey, I have to give you something."

"I can think of several things and you don't even have to go upstairs for them."

"Wouldn't compete with this choker."

"Don't sell yourself so short," his smile was playfully consoling.

County slid her foot along the sofa they shared and nudged his thigh. They had the main room to themselves later that night once everyone had turned in.

"Although...hmm..." she tapped a finger to her cheek.

"What?" he probed.

"There is one thing I've got- it's pretty amazing."

Fernando settled back to his side of the long sofa, adoring the image of his wife and preparing himself to be indulged.

"I'm pregnant."

The look he gave her then was priceless.

Fernando tried to angle himself up into a straighter position but strength was nonexistent. His hand merely rested limp on the cushion.

"Say that again," he watched her mouth as though he were dazed.

She obliged with a soft smile. "I'm pregnant."

"Is this why you've been acting like such an idiot?"

Her shrug bared a shoulder when the wide neckline of her yellow orange sweater dipped. "I've heard that idiocy is one of the side effects. Ramsey?" She'd watched him stare at her stomach for a long moment. "Are you happy?" She asked when his extraordinary gaze met hers.

A second after the words left her tongue, Fernando was pulling his wife into crushing hug. "If you think I'm anything else," his rich baritone was muffled in her neck, "you really are crazy."

The lovers held each other until the fire settled in the hearth. The heat of their embrace however was enough to rival any flame.

**

Four Days Later...

The engagement party/barbeque/baby showers went off without a hitch. Well...unless one counted the steadily falling snow that had churned up into a full blown blizzard. Nevertheless, the happy events were successful by anyone's standards. Things had taken on an even more joyous tone when Fernando and Contessa shared their news.

"I vote for extending the trip," Taurus said while adding a healthy dousing of steak sauce to his rib eye.

Kraven smiled while tilting up a frosted mug of beer. "I second that."

"I believe this'll get a unanimous vote," Melina predicted.

"Well," Ty clasped her hands, "the grandparents already said they were happy to spoil- I mean *stay* with the kids for as long as we needed them."

"Should we make this official, then?" Smoak asked once laughter over Ty's dig had eased off a bit.

"All those in favor?" Sabra prompted.

The question was followed by a unanimous round of *I*s and then a unanimous round of kisses.

As the storm raged outside; bringing the temperatures to bone chilling depths, the warmth inside went beyond that brought on by the mugs of hot tea, cocoa and mulled wine. It went beyond the fires that raged in every hearth throughout the beautifully crafted lodge and its dazzling festive décor.

It was a warmth fortified by the couples who reveled in the love and renewed strength of their unbreakable bonds.

THE END

Dear Reader,

This book would not have been written were it not for the insistent (and appreciated) requests from my awesome Ramsey and Tesano addicts during the past year.

With each new request, I realized I was being given the answer to a problem I was having with the series.

As you can tell, this story focused heavily on the couples. Clearly, the lovers had many unsettled issues still at work between them. I had been working to find a way to include and resolve their issues over the course of the next three books but I didn't feel they belonged there.

Your 'requests' got me to thinking that a Christmas book might be a nice place to have the couples hash out their lingering issues amidst a winter escape full of the love and passion you've come to expect from these sexy folks.

I hope you've enjoyed another glimpse into their lives.

With that said, I wish you all a Very Merry Christmas, Joyful Holidays and A Happy New Year.

Much Love,
AlTonya
altonya@lovealtonya.com
https://twitter.com/Ramseysgirl
http://www.facebook.com/altonyaw

An AlTonya Exclusive

Made in the USA
Lexington, KY
11 December 2012